W9-ASJ-988

About the Book

She was forbidden.

I didn't care.

As my best friend's little sister, Macey Hale was off-limits, but the girl was tempting as sin and forbidden as fuck. I wish I could say that stopped me. I wish I could tell you I behaved like a gentleman.

I didn't.

When she waltzes back into my life with that same spark I fell for, looking every bit the beautiful woman I knew she'd grow into, I have to force myself to remember I'm different from the man she once knew. I'm colder. Harder. And for good reason.

With my heart on lockdown and my hands aching to touch her, I set out to prove that I can keep myself in check this time.

No strings. No attachments.

And definitely no falling for her again.

Praise for *Sinfully Mine*

"*Sinfully Mine* is a panty-melting blend of angst, heartbreak, sex, and romance. Reece is devastatingly sexy, Macey is pure sass, and the story will make you squirm in your seat while craving more. Forbidden love with a twist of BDSM equals heat overload and a whole lot of fanning yourself. For the record, Reece is mine." – *Rachel Brookes, bestselling author of the Breathe series*

Chapter One

Reece

She's standing here as if she didn't shatter my entire world six years ago.

Blinking my eyes against what I'm sure is a mirage, or maybe too much Scotch, I address the gorgeous woman standing demurely before me. "Macey?"

I'd recognize her anywhere, but this isn't the girl I remember. I haven't seen her in years, and she's grown up. *A lot*. Her features are sharper, and she's lost the childlike roundness to her face. Her hair is longer, lighter, and her makeup is perfectly applied. I don't recall her ever wearing makeup. But mostly it's the look in her eyes that's different—as if she's seen too much of the world and had to cut her own path through it. She's harder, edgier, wiser . . . but she's still Macey. And my heart is beating like a fucking drum at the sight of her.

"Hi, Reece." Her tone is confident, but her body language doesn't match it. Her eyes are guarded, and her gaze drifts to the floor at my feet.

I fell in love with her when I was nineteen and she was sixteen. I knew it was wrong; she was my best friend's little sister. But when she lost her parents in a plane crash that year, I was the one she turned to for comfort, and our friendship evolved from there.

Of course, my best friend, Hale, doesn't know any of this because it ended when she went away to college. It had to. Macey was always destined for more, and leaving was exactly what she needed, even if she took a part of me with her.

Despite the fact that we're standing in the busy lounge of my BDSM club, Crave, I'm immediately transported back to her quiet, dim bedroom six years ago. I was twenty, with all the wants and needs of a man, and she was just an inexperienced girl of seventeen . . .

• • •

Macey's panties were wet, and her chest heaved up and down with her quick, shallow breaths.

"Are you sure about this?" I asked her.

"I'm sure," she said, her voice small but steady.

Her white cotton underwear left little to the imagination, since the now-damp fabric clung to the inviting pink skin beneath. I'd been rubbing her clit through her panties, unwilling to undress her completely because I knew what would happen once I did. Her knees were spread apart, her thin tank top unable to conceal the firm peaks of her nipples. She was beautiful—a lesson in contradictions. Shy but uninhibited; inexperienced yet eager.

She was close, whimpering softly as my fingers worked on her. My cock was so hard it ached, and all the blood pumping south clouded my judgment. Continuing to caress her, I used my free hand to release my belt and open my pants. Taking myself in my hand, I pumped my cock up and down, needing a release so fucking badly it hurt.

Macey and I both released a shuddering breath at the same moment. Her gaze was glued to my jerky movements, and I could feel all her muscles trembling.

"Do you have a condom?" she asked, a slight tremor to her words.

I had two condoms in my wallet, and as much as I wanted her, I was also scared out of my mind. I'd never slept with a woman I loved. Up until this moment, sex had been a meaningless physical act meant to quiet the need raging inside me, nothing more than joyless weekend hookups with girls whose names I wouldn't recall in the morning.

But Macey wasn't just the girl I'd grown to love, she was also my best friend's little sister and a virgin—a combination that was completely off-limits. So why was I in her bed with my cock in my hand?

I didn't answer her about the condom—not because I couldn't—but because in that moment, the only thing I wanted was to watch her come. To see her beautiful features as she lost control completely.

As I leaned down to take her mouth, her greedy tongue met mine, sucking hard as she lifted her hips slightly off the bed, pressing herself into my touch. My hand slid up and down my shaft, and I knew I was going to come soon. I kissed a path down her neck to her collarbone, making my way down her body past the dip in her belly until I settled between her thighs.

Lifting the fabric of her panties to the side, I exposed her delicate pink flesh. She was beautiful. I'd always insisted that her panties stay on while we fooled around. It was my one nonnegotiable rule, a small thing to ease my guilt. Macey opened her mouth to protest until she felt my tongue lap at her clit, and then she gave a short whimper and buried her hands in my hair, tugging me closer as her head dropped back on the pillow.

I chuckled against her skin, loving the taste of her. She tasted even better than I could have imagined. And her cunt smelled so fucking good, I wanted to bury myself inside it.

My mouth was everywhere at once, all over her sweetness, lapping up the honey of her virgin pussy, nipping at her clit gently with my teeth, licking her in a steady rhythm over and over as I squeezed the base of my cock so I wouldn't come . . .

• • •

"Reece?" she asks, drawing me back to the moment.

Fuck.

I want to ask her a million questions. How did she find me? Why is she here? What does she want?

But I'm unable to stop myself from studying her. Her skin looks so soft. I wonder if it's still lightly perfumed with lavender and honey like I remember. I want to lean close and taste her, but I don't. Control is everything to me now; it's all I have. Still, I continue to study her, amazed at the beautiful woman she's become. Long dark hair flows over her shoulders, leading to a trim waist and the gentle curve of well-rounded hips. Dressed in skinny jeans and tall boots, her shapely legs seem to go on forever.

She crosses her arms under her ample breasts, bringing attention to the fact she has a glorious rack. *Dear God. Are those Ds?*

"You've grown up," I say, my voice strained as I fight to recover from the effect she has on me.

Noting how my eyes had briefly wandered from hers, Macey smirks. "So have you. Unless my memories are off. How tall are you these days?"

"Six-four."

"God, it's been a long time." She smiles at me, but there's a faraway sadness in her eyes I don't like.

"Six years," I say, even though it wasn't a question. "Does Hale know you're here?" It's funny how my internal thoughts immediately go to him, almost like my subconscious is trying to remind me why I can't do this. Besides, something tells me her older brother wouldn't be too happy about her destination tonight. I don't even know how she found me.

Shaking her head, Macey drops her chin toward her chest. The girl I remember was confident, carefree, and sassy. This version of her is more subdued and serious, totally unlike her.

Using two fingers, I lift her chin to meet my gaze. "Who's done this to you?"

"What?" she asks, flushed and slightly breathless.

That reaction is to be expected, given our surroundings. Crave is Chicago's hottest BDSM club. But her reaction to the club isn't what I'm referring to at all.

"Who's dimmed that light in your eyes?"

She looks away, not wanting to answer.

That's the thing about Macey. Even from the

time she was a skinny little girl, those huge blue eyes were like two pools of light that swallowed you whole, sucked you into her orbit, and made you feel alive and slightly out of control.

I can't resist reaching out to touch her again, this time tucking a stray lock of chestnut-colored hair behind her ear. The urge to take her in my arms and hold her tightly flares inside me. And to say I'm not the cuddling type would be a huge fucking understatement. But this is Macey, and I really don't like seeing her like this. I want to comfort her. It's that same overwhelming feeling that came over me when her parents died. I just want to fix it.

She inhales sharply at the contact, but her gaze stays on mine. "How about a drink first?"

I nod, placing my hand against her lower back to lead the way toward the bar. After helping Macey onto the only open bar stool, I stand beside her and gesture to the bartender. Macey's trying to play it cool, but her eyes widen as her gaze darts around the club.

The first floor is relatively tame compared with what she'd find upstairs. Slate-gray velvet couches are interspersed with high-top tables and leather bar stools, places meant for mingling in small groups or more intimate one-on-one connections. The people mingling tonight are a mix of businessmen looking to cut loose, bored housewives eager for an adventure, and sex kittens wanting to experience the real-life alpha males they've only read about in popular fiction.

Muted soft grays and deep hues of blue dot the space. Soft fabrics and low lighting are meant to invite you in and get you comfortable. The deep notes of club music thumping in the background create an underlying current of raw sexual energy crackling in the air. I can feel it, and I know Macey can too.

The open floor plan is both sophisticated and sinful, a balance I've worked hard to achieve with the help of a designer, and believe me, this place makes good on its promise for hot, discreet sex.

It's New Year's Eve in the city, and Crave, as the hottest place to be, is packed tonight. It doesn't skimp on sleek, elegant décor, pricey liquor, or beautiful people. I should feel proud and elated, but instead my head is still spinning from the scene I just witnessed upstairs. I helped Hale with his new submissive, Brielle, just moments ago. She presented her tight little ass to us at his command, and even with her on display, all I could think about was getting back to Macey. I couldn't believe when my security staff called me over, pointing to the woman near the door who asked to speak with me. But before I could gather my courage to approach her, Hale called my cell, asking for backup with his scene. Of course I went. He's my best friend.

All I could think about was Macey during the scene, how Hale's fucking little sister was out there waiting for me. If anyone tried to pick her up or take her to a private room, so help me, I would rip his arms off and beat him with them. And since that would be bad for business, I was hoping it didn't come to that.

Hale would freak out if he knew she was here, so I kept things brief and stayed quiet about that fact, playing the part he expected of me before slipping out of the room to return to her. And now that I'm standing with her, I'm speechless once again.

The bar is packed, given that it's New Year's Eve, and we watch the bartender filling drink orders and slinging bottles for a couple of quiet moments.

"Why don't you start out by telling me exactly why you came here tonight?" I ask. Last I knew, Macey had been living in Miami.

"Let me give you a hint." She leans closer, letting the weight of her generous breasts brush against my chest as she bends close to my ear. "My personal life went to shit, and now I need hot, sweaty sex. I need forget-my-own-name sex."

The sweet little Macey I remember has left the building, folks.

My cock hardens instantly.

I can't even blame it on teenage hormones like I could back then. My attraction to her has always been a powerful, dangerous thing, hell-bent on getting me in trouble. I've had way too many fantasies of pounding into her tight, hot cunt. I've jacked off countless times to that image, as wrong as it is.

Just then, the bartender saunters up and asks what we're craving, a little tagline my publicity company came up with. All the bar staff and waitresses have been trained to use it.

Having not spent any time with the adult version of Macey, I have no idea what she drinks, so I'm surprised when she orders herself a whiskey, neat. Something in me likes that she's not a fruity-drink type of girl. Her personality is straightforward and intoxicating, and her drink choice reflects it. It's a hell of a woman who drinks whiskey straight up, or maybe she's more thrown off at seeing me than she's letting on. I sure as fuck am.

Once we've settled in with our drinks, her gaze lands on me again. "So it's true then."

"What's true?" I ask before swallowing a mouthful of Scotch.

"That you own this place."

I give her a nod. No sense in denying it. Besides, I'm proud of what I've built for myself. I worked hard to raise enough capital, made some smart investments, and have worked my ass off to make this place a reality.

She bites her lip as she toys with her glass, then brings her gaze back to me. "When I got into town tonight and Cameron wasn't answering his phone, I Googled you."

Watching her expression, I'm trying to read her, knowing she's thinking I never had a penchant for kink when she and I were together. But I'm not explaining the reason why to her. Not now, and hopefully not ever. My way of life has worked for me, and I don't want to change it. I keep my heart on lockdown, a willing submissive on speed dial, and my dick wet. It's all good.

Curiosity edges out my better judgment. "How long will you be in town?"

"For good," she says, surprising me with the defiance in those big blue eyes. "I left my job, left my cheating ex-boyfriend, packed everything I owned, and here I am."

Damn.

Macey worked as a newscaster for a Latin TV station in Miami. She double-majored in Spanish and journalism in college, earning both degrees ahead of schedule. She's smart and driven, and ambitious. Which is why it surprises me to hear her say she's just thrown in the towel on it all.

"I'm sorry to hear that." It explains the sadness radiating from her that I picked up on earlier. "So, what's on your agenda now, other than the hot, sweaty pounding you mentioned?"

Looking up at me through her eyelashes, she murmurs, "Why don't you finish that drink first, and I'll tell you."

I don't know if it's the alcohol or the erotic

atmosphere that has loosened her up, but she's more carefree now, becoming positively playful. "Are you trying to get me liquored up, Macey?"

"And what if I was?" A slow, sassy smile uncurls on her mouth.

Holy fuck. This girl is going to be trouble; I can tell in an instant. The flirting. The drinks. She's trying to push me into action. Topping from the bottom.

So Macey wants a big bad Dom to show her the ropes? I should paddle her ass for showing up here tonight. But this can't be like six years ago where I lose my shit completely, only to have her waltz out of town again when the next opportunity pops up.

Chapter Two

Macey

God, I hate how seeing Reece transports me right back to that shy eighteen-year-old girl I once was—the one who fell hard and fast for her older brother's best friend, only to have him suddenly end things right before I left for college. Back then, the naive me wanted to tell him everything, to admit the extent of my feelings and then come clean to my brother about my relationship with Reece. I wanted take things to the next level, one that existed in the light of day instead of sneaking around behind closed doors.

Of course, none of that happened because he broke things off before I ever got the chance. The heartache wasn't as bad as losing my parents, but it was damn close. Reece meant everything to me back then.

I spent my whole first semester at college floating around in a fog. That's what led me to double majoring. I filled my schedule so completely I had no time to sit around and feel sorry for myself. And I guess it worked because I eventually got over Reece, graduated early and with honors, and then moved on and dated other men. It all felt like I was just going through the motions, but somehow the years passed and I moved on.

But as I look up into his hungry dark eyes, I know none of it is true. Apparently I've never really moved on at all, because when things in my life fell apart again, he's the one I ran to.

I knock back my drink in a single gulp, because heaven help me, I need some brass lady balls for what I'm about to do. It's a new year and a fresh start for me, and I'm grabbing what I want and running with it. No regrets. Life's too damn short.

Showing up on New Year's probably wasn't my smartest move. Of course, my brother is out somewhere, probably drunk or worse after what that skank of an ex-fiancée did to him. So that left me with staying with either Nana or Reece. And considering I didn't want to wake up an eighty-year-old woman, I typed REECE JACKSON into Google and closed my eyes, praying for a search result and that he was home tonight.

What I got instead shook me to my core. Apparently, twenty-seven-year-old Reece Jackson is the multimillionaire owner of Chicago's hottest underground sex club. I never would have pegged him for a Dominant, but it makes sense. He's always been intense and demanding. I just can't believe Cameron never mentioned it all the times I asked about Reece.

He's even more devastatingly handsome than I recall. He's tall, masculine, and extremely fit. His dark hair is cut short, with just enough to grab onto. He still has the features I remember, but now they seem more refined. Some things are definitely new, though. Dark tattoos hidden behind the sleeve of his shirt, circling his wrist, suggest a sleeve decorating his arm. I want to see more. He never had a single tattoo when I knew him. He's the man I measured all others against, and the reason no one has ever measured up.

Reece lifts his drink to his mouth and looks at me over the rim of the glass. I know he's noticed me checking him out, but he doesn't call me out. "You want to talk about the ex-douche?" he asks, his voice a harsh growl.

"Tony?" I snort. "Not particularly."

"Humor me, Pancake. I need to understand this."

I let out a deep sigh. I haven't heard that name in years. He's called me Pancake since that one morning in my parents' kitchen when, in my overexcitement of watching a sleep-rumpled Reece lumber down the stairs, I dropped the mixing bowl on the floor, sending gooey batter flying in every direction.

Reece didn't even falter. He walked straight up to me, wiped a smear of batter off my cheek, and brought it to his mouth. "Mmm. Banana?"

I merely nodded, frozen in place. Banana

chocolate chip pancakes were his favorite back then, and I made them every chance I got.

He bent down to pick up the bowl and cleaned up while I started a new batch. We worked as a good team, even back then. And I'm wondering if we still do.

"Macey? The ex?" Reece interrupts my little daydream. "Is there someone's ass I need to fly down to Florida to kick?"

Just thinking about Tony agitates me. Having to actually talk about him makes me boiling angry.

Reece signals the bartender. "Another of those?" he asks, reading my mood.

I give him a tight nod. "Might help."

The busty redheaded bartender wearing a leather corset gives Reece a flirty wink, then sets the drink down in front of me with an unceremonious thud. I don't want to explore the flash of jealousy that surges through me.

Reece is still watching me, still waiting for me

to answer.

I take a small sip, appreciating the bite of the liquor as it sinks all the way to my belly and warms me. "We dated for nine months. He was between jobs much of that time, and so he moved in with me about six months ago. Last week I came home from work early and caught him banging the living daylights out of our landlord, Pinky."

"Is Pinky a man or a woman?" he asks.

"Does it matter?" I press my lips together.

"Not really." He shrugs. "I'm just trying to follow along."

"Pinky is a fifty-eight-year-old woman." There's nothing like a slap to the face or your self-confidence than finding your boyfriend balls deep inside a grandmother. *Fuck my life.*

"Damn, Macey." Reece shakes his head. "You're beautiful and sexy, and deserve much more than that. I'd say you dodged a fucking bullet with that guy. He's obviously a total fuckwit."

I smile, despite myself. Maybe it's being in the presence of Reece, or maybe it's the liquor, but I'm feeling better than I have in days.

"Yeah. I'm just ready to move on." And it's the truth. I wasn't in love with Tony, but we lived together and were in a committed, monogamous relationship, or at least I was. But that's over now.

"And your job?" he asks.

"The station was downsizing. I saw the writing on the wall." I shrug.

"And so you're here."

"I am." I don't know if he means here as in Crave, or here as in Chicago, but doubt creeps in. "I'm sorry I just showed up like this. My intention was to go to Cam's for the night. Figure out my next move after that. But it's New Year's and I wasn't thinking. Of course, he's not home. I'm sure he's out on the town."

"He's upstairs, actually."

Shock slams into me. "He's *here*?"

"Uh . . ."

I've never see Reece speechless before, but several minutes of awkward silence follow before he manages a response.

"Shit. I shouldn't have assumed you knew about his membership here."

"He's a *member*?" I can't even. My straitlaced attorney of a brother is into BDSM? *What in the actual fuck?*

"Dammit." Reece curses under his breath before signaling the big-breasted bartender for another. "Yeah. Sorry to burst your innocence bubble."

I take a deep, calming breath, realizing I've been staring at him with wide eyes and a look of shock frozen on my face. "Actually, that's what I'm hoping you'll help me with."

"What's that?"

With my pulse pounding and my hands trembling, I pull back my shoulders and look straight into his eyes. "Six years ago, you stopped things before we got to the main event."

He licks his lips. Lips that are full and demanding, yet soft. Lips that once did wicked things to my body. "It was the right thing to do."

Although I disagree, I don't argue because I'm thinking over my strategy. I'm no quitter. I've lusted after Reece Jackson for at least a decade, and now I'm single and living in the same city as him again. After the hell Tony put me through, it's time to have some fun. I didn't expect to learn Reece owned a BDSM club, but if I'm honest, I have to admit it only makes me more curious. *When in Rome . . .*

He's always been that unobtainable older guy—my brother's best friend—and now the knowledge that he knows his way around a toy box only has my body humming that much more. The memories of our years together haunt me; we still have unfinished business.

I set out to prove to him that I would make

something of myself after he cast me aside. But all roads led right back to where I started. *Reece*. I can't help but remember the night I almost lost my virginity—or rather, my failed attempt at it.

Him with a large bulge in his pants. Me with my panties pulled to the side while I fingered myself, trying to tempt him. The pained expression on his face as he watched.

I ache just thinking about it. I felt rejected and ridiculous. Shit, I still do. All of it rushes back through me like it was just yesterday. It's time to let go of the past and make some new memories.

Glancing around the club, I take in its secretive, sexual allure, and the desire to be a bit reckless nudges at me. I meet Reece's eyes as the familiar powerful chemistry crackles between us. "I'm here because I want to experience this."

"What exactly do you want to *experience*?" he asks, his eyes narrowing.

"You tell me, you're the Dom." I fight off a

sassy smile, trying not to taunt him. "I told you. I've just come out of a less-than-ideal situation, and all I want is sex—no, *good* sex—and a few orgasms to forget my own damn name."

"And how does this involve me, Macey?"

My heart sinks a little. I'll admit, this is random. I get that. I haven't seen or spoken to Reece in years. But he owns a sex club. Clearly there's no better man for the job.

"You own a sex club, for fuck's sake. Are you really going to be a prude about this?"

He stiffens and leans back a little. "Excuse me if I'm a little fucking thrown off, Pancake. I haven't seen you in what, six years? And now you just expect me to whip out my flogger and spank you?"

I chew on my lip. *Now we're talking.* "Or your cock," I suggest helpfully.

"I need to talk to Hale."

My eyes widen, and I snort out a nervous laugh. "You're going to discuss this with my brother? Are you insane?" He's always called Cameron by our last name. Most of his close friends do, in fact. But discussing this with my brother is not a fucking good idea.

He smirks, and damn if it isn't sexy. "Probably a little, but we're doing things different this time."

Why is it that any reference to our history sends a little stabbing pain through my chest? That needs to stop. "Different how?"

"We're playing by my rules." His fist tightens at his side, making the veins stand out on his tattooed forearm.

As I study him, taking in the stiffness to his shoulders and the hard set of his jaw, I realize this Reece is a different man from the one I remember. He's forceful and edgier with a new intensity simmering just under the surface. It makes me want to peel back each and every layer, and discover all I've been missing.

To be fair, I've changed a lot too. I've learned a

lot these past few years while building a career and making a name for myself. Mostly, I learned that confidence is the key to getting what you want. I'd used the mantra *fake it 'til you make it* more than once at my job back in Miami. And now it seems I need to use it to land Reece too.

This time around I'm going to be the one taking what I want. No cheating ex or crappy job is going to tell me good-bye. I'm going to take my pleasure and ride the wave of my naughtiest adventure all the way to Screaming Orgasmville. First stop: How to Become a Submissive 101.

Reece interrupts my thoughts, softening his voice. "How about a tour of the club?" He tips his head toward the lounge. "If you're still interested after you know what you'd be getting into, then we'll talk."

Given that I've only seen the entrance and now the bar, of course I'm curious about this place I've found myself in. "Sure."

Taking one last swig of my drink, I leave the

glass at the bar and follow his lead.

His hand comes to rest against my lower back, just above my butt, sending tingles zipping up and down my spine. In my skinny jeans and simple cotton tunic, I'm way underdressed compared to the other women here. From another perspective, I may be overdressed given that most of the women are parading around in body-hugging cocktail dresses or skimpy lingerie, leaving little to the imagination. But having the undivided attention of the best-looking man in the place makes me feel like a goddess.

Reece guides me away from the bar and toward a staircase. As we climb the stairs to the second floor, my belly dances with nerves. Maybe he's right; maybe I won't like what I see here and I'll run away. Part of me thinks that's exactly what he wants. I can't let that happen.

Upstairs is a long hallway with several rooms on either side. Reece walks slowly in front of me and I follow, hating how my gaze keeps dropping to his incredibly tight butt. *Focus, Macey.*

A peek inside the first room only serves as a reminder that I shouldn't have left my whiskey at the bar. Because, *holy shit*, there's a naked woman strapped to a table. A man and a woman are leaned over her, each sucking on a breast while another man uses a large handheld massager on her fun bits as he strokes himself.

Fucking A! I didn't know clubs like this really existed, that *people* like this really existed. I spend most Saturday nights with a pizza and my remote—thank you, Netflix—and apparently I am really freaking sheltered.

"You okay?" Reece's voice is low and calm, as if he's completely unaffected by the orgy happening just three feet from us.

The scent of sex in the air makes me dizzy, and I can practically feel the hum of the vibrator, as though it's being used on me. Straightening my shoulders, I fix my best sultry expression on my face. "Absolutely fine."

Pretending that I'm not completely thrown off, and geez, kind of horny, I follow him farther down the hall, wondering what else is in store for me.

Next up is a medical exam room where a woman is probing a man who's lying on the table, his feet in the stirrups. I probably didn't need to see that. Quite a role reversal, though, and I appreciate that. Ten points for creativity. Next we watch two women who role-play a scene that involves spanking with a little whip thingy. My breath catches in my throat.

"It's called a riding crop," Reece leans over and whispers.

"Does it hurt?" Given the way the woman being spanked is leaning into it and moaning tells me no, but I don't know if I trust her judgment. These people could all be half-crazy for all I know.

"Depends on how it's used." His answer is coy, frustrating me since it tells me nothing about the toy or about his preferences for play. Of course, it only makes me more curious. Maybe that was his intention all along.

As we continue the tour, Reece points to a series of closed doors at the far end of the hall. "Those are the private rooms for people who don't want to put on a show, and want to experience something more intimate."

"And what about you? Which of these rooms do you prefer to play in?"

"Depends on who I'm with. If my partner is more of an exhibitionist, or if I think the experience of being watched will push her outside her comfort zone, we might play in one of the common rooms. But for the most part, I tend to be a closed-door kind of guy."

Studying him for a moment, I try to digest everything I've just seen and reconcile it with the teenaged Reece I remember. I come up short; it just doesn't compute. How the hell did he get from there to here?

"Care to fill me in on the last six years? I mean,

this is quite a detour from the man I knew."

He shrugs. "There's really nothing to tell. I have certain needs and interests. And when I couldn't find a place to satisfy all of those interests, I opened my own."

"How did you get this way?" I wince a little, not meaning to blurt it out like an accusation, then soften my voice. "I just don't remember you ever having this fetish side to you."

His gaze darkens, telling me he's hiding something from me. It makes me wonder; Cameron never mentioned anything out of the ordinary. Anytime I asked about Reece, my brother would merely give me a noncommittal grunt, and when I pushed and asked if Reece was seeing anyone, Cam's reluctant response was always, "Several."

I'm really not sure what to make of this new revelation that Reece owns this place, that he lives and breathes BDSM, but I'm trying to loosen up and go with it. It's exactly what I need to push all the depressing thoughts from my brain. It's the ultimate distraction, perfectly timed.

"Come on. You've probably had a long day," he says, offering me his hand.

"Where are we going?" I place my palm in his. His skin is warm, and an intoxicating male scent greets me as I get closer, some type of upscale men's cologne. *Yummy*.

"Do you have anywhere to stay tonight?"

I shake my head. "I was planning to get a hotel room somewhere."

"It's almost midnight. You probably won't be able to get a cab or a hotel room at this hour. Come on. You can stay in my apartment. It's upstairs."

"I could just stay down here, see if I can find someone to entertain myself with." After what I've just witnessed, I'm sure that won't be difficult. Shit, it might even be fun.

He grips my hand tightly, and his reaction gives me a little spurt of confidence. "The hell you will.

You're going to bed."

Pulling my hand away, I plant both hands on my hips and meet his icy stare. "I'm not tired."

"Too damn bad. I don't want to have to worry about you."

"This isn't like when we were kids, Reece."

"You think I don't know that? You're *all* woman and that's exactly why I'm not leaving you down here alone. It'd be like throwing you to the wolves."

"Maybe I want a little trouble." I raise my eyebrows suggestively.

He leans in closer. "Or I can tell Hale where you are."

Point taken. Changing tack, I ask, "Do you have a bathtub?"

His puzzled expression betrays his confusion. "I do."

"Fine, let's go. I think I'll take a hot soak. I've

been traveling all day."

I follow him to the elevator, where he inserts a special key and hits a button for the top floor. No wonder this address came up when I searched for him. It's not only his business, but also his residence. Reece has really submersed himself in this world, and I wish I understood more about it and the man he's morphed into while I've been away.

"You never answered my question," I say, finally feeling the full effects of the alcohol. I'm drowsy and tipsy, and liable to say anything right about now.

"And what question was that?" His voice is way too in control, and it's annoying me.

"You. Me." I lift one eyebrow.

"You're going to have to be more specific."

Fuck it. Throwing caution to the wind, I lick my lips, noting the way his eyes follow the movement. "About you, pounding into me from behind. Me, screaming out your name."

"I told you. I need to talk to Hale."

"And say what?" I shoot back.

"I'm not doing this again without his blessing."

"Nothing happened." Nothing but a broken heart and six long years of mourning what could have been. For me it was young love, but to him it's ancient history, if the brash tone of the man before me is any indicator.

"Enough happened."

The elevator jerks to a stop, and when the doors open I follow him down a dimly lit hallway, the bite of rejection stinging with each step I take.

He walks in front of me and when he glances back, I wish I could read his expression. Aside from the tic of his jaw and set of his posture, he gives away nothing. Maybe it was a mistake coming here.

When he unlocks the door and lets us inside, it's like I've tripped a live explosive, because Reece pushes my back against the wall and his lips crash down on mine. His mouth is hot, demanding, and needy, speaking a language I readily comprehend.

Every nerve ending in my body hums to life at once. *Yes, yes, yes.* This is why I came here, this right here. His presence alone forces every stray thought from my brain so I can just feel. I kiss him back, licking against his tongue, unable to help the small mewling cries that escape me as I press my body close to his.

He pulls away suddenly, making me mourn the loss of his firm body looming over mine. "Some things have changed since you've been gone," he says tightly. "*If* we do this, you will play by my rules. There will be no topping from the bottom. Your wrists will be bound by my ropes. That hot, tight cunt will be wrapped around my cock, and you won't come until I say."

My knees tremble, and my breath catches in my throat. *Please. Yes, to all of that. Times one hundred.*

"I understand, sir," I murmur.

That word does interesting things to him. His

pupils dilate and he forces his mouth on mine again, sucking on my tongue, and grips my ass roughly through my jeans. My center turns molten and my panties go damp.

"Fuck. You still taste so good. Just like I remember." He pulls his lips from mine and lands a sharp swat against my ass.

"Ouch." I rub the tender cheek. "What was that for?"

"For giving me this when I have to go back to work." His hand drops down to grip the bulge at the front of his pants.

My, my. I giggle. "Sorry."

"Come on. I have a guest room." He leads me into a bedroom down the hall furnished only with a large bed with crisp white sheets and a gray duvet. "Is this okay?"

"Yes." I look around. I only have my purse, having left all my bags in my car, which is parked several blocks away.

"Something to sleep in?" he asks.

"Please."

He returns moments later holding a Chicago Cubs T-shirt. It's soft and faded from numerous washings, its original navy color now more of a muted blue. It's perfect. "Thank you."

"The bathroom is at the end of the hall, and the towels are in the cabinet under the sink."

I sit down on the edge of the bed, tired and confused. My attraction to him is even stronger than I imagined it could be after all these years, and I'm not sure what to make of that. This was supposed to be daring and fun. It wasn't supposed conjure up a bunch of memories and what-ifs.

Reece gazes at me as if he's cataloging all the ways I've changed over the years. Without saying a word, he stalks closer and takes my hand. My nails are polished jet black, my signature color lately, and he looks displeased somehow.

"This is new," he says at last.

I pull my hand away and nod toward his tattooed arm that I've only caught glimpses of. "So is that."

He nods. "So it is."

As he studies me with those dark eyes again, I'm unnerved. Things have changed between us. We have changed. And I have no idea if we still fit together. It's a thought that depresses me.

"Are you sure it's okay that I'm here?" I ask.

"Of course. You'll be safe here. I promise. The elevator only works with my key, and I'm the only one with a copy. And I'll lock the dead bolt to the front door when I leave."

"No, I just meant I don't want to complicate things for you." I hadn't even thought to ask if he was dating someone.

"Just let me figure some things out, okay?"

I nod, understanding that he's not going to sidestep Hale this time. We're both adults now, and even if I'm annoyed, I appreciate that he's acting like a grown man.

"Get some rest, okay?" He pulls the blankets down on the side of the bed, as if he's going to tuck me in.

"You can't stay?" I was kind of hoping we could talk, catch up more.

"It's one of the busiest nights of the year for the club. I need to make sure everyone stays safe and has fun."

How responsible of him. I'm not sure what I expected when I showed up here tonight. Part of me hoped we'd drop our pants and hump like bunnies, but to be honest, I like this grown-up, mature adult version of Reece. He's going to make sure things are right first, pave the way for us before we begin. It already feels more serious than I counted on.

"Okay. I'll see you later then."

He leans in toward me and plants a soft kiss on my lips. "Happy New Year, Pancake."

"Happy New Year."

The air feels full of new beginnings and promises to explore. Only I'm not sure if that's a good thing or a bad thing.

Chapter Three

Reece

I must have a death wish, because this lunch is likely to end with my homicide. Hale and I are sitting in our favorite bistro, our food growing cold in front of us.

When Macey strolled so casually back into my life, I was thrown. But only for a moment, because now I have a plan. She wants to play? Fine. I'll play the game, but this time she'll be playing by my rules.

Hale seems distracted; he keeps checking his phone for some reason.

"Do you have something going on?" I ask, taking a tentative bite of my sandwich.

He shakes his head. "No, just reading a message from Brielle." His mouth forms into a silly grin. *The bastard.*

I sigh, setting my food aside. I never thought I'd see the day Cameron Hale fell in love. I can use this to my advantage. Maybe his softer side will triumph, and he won't want to kill me when I tell him what I came here to say. Still, I decide to stall, like the pussy I am.

"How are things between you and Brielle? The other night was pretty intense." I can't help but remember the way her eyes followed him around the room, as if he was her answer to life's every question.

"She's it for me. I've been burned in the past, and I know you probably think I'm insane, but I'm going to ask her to marry me."

Whoa. "Not insane at all. Even a blind man could have seen the love between you two. I'm happy for you. Besides, Brielle is nothing like that super-whore Tara."

He grunts. He doesn't like to talk about Tara, but he knows I'm right. They're worlds apart. Brielle is sweet and thoughtful and kind. Tara only saw Hale as her personal bank account. I'm pretty sure she zeroed in on him when she found out about the trust his parents left him, like a cheetah stalking a gazelle.

"How was the rest of the night? The club was packed," Hale remarks.

"Yeah, business was great. We made a killing, and new memberships have been pouring in since the event. My office staff is working overtime just to keep up with the demand."

"Congratulations." He lifts his water glass to mine.

"Thanks, man." When I opened this club three years ago, I could have never imagined the success I've found. Apparently, sex sells. And well.

We eat in comfortable silence for a few minutes while I contemplate what I came here to talk to him about. *Macey.* Why am I going to bat for her? Because as much as I hate to admit it, we have unfinished business between us. She left me with the worst blue balls and a broken heart years ago. It's time to settle the score.

"How's Macey doing?" I ask, like I don't know firsthand.

She's been back for two days, already hunting

for an apartment in the city. I think she planned to stay with her brother, but given that he has a roommate, and I'm guessing he's going to be moving on to live with Brielle soon, it's left Macey to fend for herself. Not that she minds. She's a tough cookie.

"How did you know she was back?" he asks with a stunned look on his face.

Shit.

I definitely can't tell him she's been staying in my guest room for the past two nights. She left this morning to go look at apartments and secondhand furniture with her nana.

"She came by the club."

"What? When?"

I take a deep breath, working up the courage for what I'm about to tell him. "New Year's Eve."

"Seriously? Why didn't you tell me? How did she even know about the club?"

"She said when she got into town and you weren't home, she Googled me, and that's what came up. Remember when security called me that night to meet up with a woman who was asking for me?"

"Holy shit. That was when you were helping me with Brielle."

I nod. "Yeah, I know."

"So, what the fuck happened?"

My gut twists painfully. *Dammit*. Food was a bad idea. I should have thought this through. I'm about to tell her damn brother that she came in demanding sex. This is not my finest moment.

"She's just come off a bad breakup, as you know, and she wants ..." My voice cracks and I cough, clearing my throat.

"She wants what?" Hale's eyes narrow on mine, etching lines across his forehead.

I force some confidence into my voice, standing my ground. She's an adult now, I remind myself. "She wants to experience BDSM."

"The fuck she does." The vein in his neck throbs as realization crosses his features. "And what, I suppose you're going to train her?" He barks out a laugh, but there's no humor in his tone.

I say nothing, but I meet his eyes and tip my head.

Hale tenses, lowering his voice to a dangerous tone. "There's no fucking way. She's a good girl, Reece. She—just no. Absolutely no. My answer is no."

"She wants to learn, Hale. She's eager."

"For the fuck of fuck. Don't tell me how *eager* my little sister is. You realize I'm three seconds away from punching you in the crotch, yes?"

"What if I showed her . . . without sexual contact?"

"Two seconds." His fists tighten at his sides, and I stifle the urge to shield my manhood.

Summoning my courage, I lean forward, resting my elbows on the table. "Just listen. If I don't show her, you and I both know she's determined enough to venture out on her own. This is Macey we're talking about, the girl who tried to join Boy Scouts because you and I were in it. The girl who in sixth grade built an entire empire of lemonade stands with locations all over the damn city. You know how headstrong she is. Do you really want her at another club, with another Dom who doesn't know a flogger from a bullwhip working with her?"

He growls out some unintelligible sound.

"I didn't think so." *Ya fucktard.*

Hale may not like it, but I know he trusts me. The Dom training Macey should be me, whether either of us likes it or not.

"No sexual contact." He pins me with an icy stare.

I raise my hands in mock defense. "Wouldn't dream of it, brother." *Except for every fucking night.* But I can't help it what my brain thinks about when I'm unconscious.

"I fucking mean it, Reece." He still looks seconds away from punching me, but my small victory lifts my spirits.

"You know . . . ," I say, my fingers tapping my chin. "Inherently, a Dom/sub relationship is sexual, whether we're, you know, doing the dirty or not." I lift one eyebrow.

"I know that. Which is why I hate this entire conversation."

"I'm just saying, you know Macey, she's not going to go for some watered-down lesson where nothing's ventured and nothing's gained. She'll leave and find herself a real Dom if I don't do this right."

"Christ." He rubs his hands across his face. "You show her the basics. But no penetration. Do not fuck my sister," he repeats slowly, his tone dead serious.

"Got it." I smirk, feeling like I've just won the damn state lottery.

"Careful, asshole. You're walking a very thin line. That's my goddamn little sister," he growls.

As if I didn't know that.

"One more thing. I—uh, might have let it slip that you're a member of the club."

"God-fucking-dammit, Reece."

"Sorry, dude." I try to look contrite, but I almost want to laugh at the expression on his face. It's a mix between someone kicked his puppy and he's going to strangle me.

"Thanks for lunch." I toss down a couple of twenties and get the fuck out of there before he can change his mind. Plus, I'm eager to get back to the club and see Macey.

Chapter Four

Macey

When Reece left this morning, saying he had business to attend to, I wasn't expecting him home just a couple of hours later. So when he arrives and finds me dancing around his apartment in a pair of yoga pants and an old T-shirt, I let out a squeal of surprise.

He holds up both hands, a grin tugging up his sexy mouth. "Sorry to startle you."

"No, it's . . . okay." I pull my earbuds from my ears, aware I'm talking entirely too loudly.

His gaze slowly moves down my body, sliding over my curves before coming to a rest on my face. "Keep yourself busy, did you?"

"Something like that."

He surveys the apartment, taking in my handiwork. His apartment is gorgeous with its tall ceilings and modern furniture. But it had all the distinct makings of a bachelor pad, so I busied myself with correcting that today in my free time.

His brow furrows and his mouth eases down from a smile into more of a grimace. *Shit.* I hadn't given two thoughts about tidying up and organizing. Nana and I were supposed to spend the morning looking at apartments, but I fell in love with the first place we saw, put a deposit down, and was back early. And a bored Macey with nothing to do is a dangerous thing.

Reece's apartment was clean but it was lacking in organization, so I straightened his bookshelves, cleaned out old leftovers from his fridge, and organized all of his *Economist* magazines by order of date, leaving them stacked neatly near his armchair. Then I tackled the closets, de-cluttering and taming the mess that's accumulated from him living as a bachelor for so many years.

I hadn't realized that he'd be mad, but the look on his face says that he is. I've invaded his personal space. *He's invited you to sleep in the guest room, not flounce around like you own the damn place.*

"I'm sorry," I blurt.

After surveying the living spaces, he heads toward his bedroom with me quick on his heels. I'm worried he's going to explode when he sees what I've done in there.

He stops and stands in the doorway. I've moved his writing desk under the window, and switched the tall bookcase to a narrow wall between the doors to his closet and bathroom. It just fits better on that wall. More feng shui.

After a brief and silent pause, Reece heads into the large walk-in closet and looks over the rows of clothes.

"Did you face all my hangers the same way?"

"Yes, and I organized your shirts by color family. See?" I point to the white shirts that lead to the gray, light blue, then navy, and finally black shirts at the back.

"Why?" He turns to face me, his expression

quizzical.

"I'm sorry, I . . . I was just trying to be helpful. We can put everything back if you like. Well, except for those Thai leftovers in the fridge. Those are long gone." Down the garbage disposal, along with the scent of aged curry. *Gross.*

He nods thoughtfully, his face a stern mask. "I don't even remember the last time I had Thai food." His fingertips skim over the rows of hanging shirts.

"Oh, and I picked you up a bath mat, because you didn't have one."

He turns to face me, his expression impassive. "Did you find an apartment today?"

"Yes. Not far from here, actually. It's in Lincoln Park. They have a third-floor unit open now, so I put a deposit down and can move in a couple of days. I need a bed, a couch, and dishes, pretty much everything. It sucks starting over."

I don't want to think about the fact that the dirtbag Tony got all of my hard-earned things in the breakup, simply because I couldn't afford to ship it all across the country. And while furnishing a new apartment will cost me almost as much, I can do it at my own pace, and my stuff won't be tainted by sour memories.

Reece exits the closet, and I follow him back out to the living room. "I'll help you move whenever you're ready." He thumbs through his stack of magazines and cocks an eyebrow at me.

Embarrassed, I glance away. They're now organized by issue date. I seriously feel like an idiot for going through all of his stuff. My intention wasn't to snoop, just to keep myself busy. I'll need to look for a job sooner than I realized.

I can only dodge Cameron's questions for so long about which friend I've been staying with. I've been vague up until this point, knowing he won't take the news well that I've been sleeping down just down the hall from Reece. He's always been the consummate older brother, concerned and overprotective, even more so after our parents passed.

When I sit down on the couch, Reece settles across from me in his leather armchair. "I talked to Hale about your request."

A flash of nerves hits my belly. I can only imagine how that conversation went. I'd have literally died of embarrassment if I'd been present for that conversation. "What did he say?"

He licks his lips and a crooked smile forms on his mouth. "If it weren't for him being madly in love with Brielle, I'm fairly certain I'd have ended up in the hospital."

I chew on my lip. My brother? In love? I'll need more information on that soon. "That bad?"

"No, actually. He agreed that you and I could work together on exploring BDSM." His gaze skitters away from mine, and he's entirely too calm. Not to mention, it doesn't sound like something Cam would agree to. Like ever.

He's leaving something out.

"That's it? He was fine with it?" My voice reveals my disbelief.

"The only caveat is there will be no sex."

I glare at him as if he's grown three heads. That's the point. The *entire* fucking point. "Are you fucking kidding me?" I don't whether to laugh or to cry. "That's the most ridiculous thing I've ever heard." There's no way in fuck I'm agreeing to that, but I don't want to shoot myself in the foot before we even begin. "Cam's an idiot," I say instead, waiting to feel him out.

Reece shrugs. "He's your older brother. It's to be expected."

"So . . . how do we do this?" *Do I drop my pants here, or are we venturing down into the club?*

"It'll be three lessons. I think you'll be satisfied with that."

My heart hammers wildly in my chest at the knowledge we're actually going to do this. Three lessons. With Reece Jackson, the Dominant. "When do we start?"

"Tonight. I have work to do today, but we'll

have dinner and discuss your goals and limits. Do you like Cuban food?"

I level him with my stare. "I lived in Miami for two years. Of course I do."

"Perfect. There's a good restaurant we can meet at tonight just down the street. The food is excellent, and the lighting is low. It's quiet enough to talk, but loud enough to not be overheard."

"Okay," I agree.

"Give me your phone."

"Why?"

"I always exchange numbers with submissives I'm working with."

He says it so dismissively, as if I'm nothing more than one of his playthings, as if we don't have a deep and complicated history. I hand my phone over reluctantly, probably some leftover reaction from Tony's constant distrust and questions. He used to read my texts, even though I was nothing but faithful to him.

Glancing at me curiously, Reece adds, "And I'm going to text you the address of the restaurant."

"All right. Sounds good. I'll see you there."

"Seven o'clock. Don't be late, Macey."

"Wouldn't dream of it, sir." I can't help the sass in my voice. One way or another, I will get my way.

Chapter Five

Reece

When I got home and saw what Macey had done to my apartment, she thought I was mad, but I was actually kind of in awe. I've never had a girlfriend, never had someone who cared enough to spend her time doing little things just for me. Thoughtful things like organizing and tidying up my place. Facing all my damn hangers the same way. Or making sure I had a soft, fluffy rug to step out on after showering, versus the cold tile that I was used to.

I'm just glad she didn't find my stash of toys. I can only imagine the butt plugs would be organized by size, the vibrators by color and intensity. A little bit of chaos in life is a good thing. Not to mention, I don't want to scare her off before we even begin. She might be putting on a brave face, but I know that I'll be opening her up to a whole new world. I could smell the fear and uncertainty on her during that club tour as if she was wearing it like a perfume.

Needing to keep busy before our meeting tonight, I find myself in my office down on the main floor of the club, catching up on business. As I gaze at my laptop screen, I realize I've been staring at the same blank spreadsheet for twenty minutes. *Shit*. I'm not even sure what I'm hoping to accomplish right now, just that I can't hang around upstairs with Macey so close in my personal space. It's throwing me off my fucking game, but I intend to get back control tonight.

"Hey, boss." Chrissy, the club sub, pokes her head in my office doorway.

"Hey, Chrissy. Everything all right?"

"Yeah. Just worried about you."

"Me?" I've never given my employees a reason to worry about me, and I don't plan to start now.

She tilts her head, examining me. "You've been different since that girl arrived."

"Macey?"

She nods. "That's the one. Unless you're hiding another woman upstairs in your apartment . . ."

"No. I'm fine. You don't have to worry."

"You don't let women stay over, though, so I assume she's someone you're serious about, but I've never heard you talk about her before."

"She and I go way back, and I'm trying to figure out how she fits into my life here, if it all."

Chrissy lets herself in and sinks into the chair across from me. She and I have a long history, mostly just as friends, though there were a few times when she first began coming to the club that we shared more. Now she's an employee, and call me old-fashioned, but I don't fuck my employees. Chrissy's a good girl, and we look out for each other.

"She used to be your submissive?" she asks, a look of concern crossing her features.

"No. We knew each other ages ago. She's not

into the lifestyle."

Chrissy smiles at me warmly. "She wouldn't be here if she wasn't interested."

That's the problem, though. I don't know if she's interested in me, curious about what goes on behind closed doors, or simply running from a crappy situation and grasping onto the first distraction she can find. I intend to find out.

Chrissy's gaze softens, and she leans in closer. "In all the time I've known you, you've never had a girlfriend, never taken on a submissive as your own."

Narrowing my eyes, I lean back in my chair. "And? Your point is?" My annoyance is rising by the second. I don't appreciate people meddling in my personal life.

"Behind the tough Dom exterior, I know you're actually a sweet guy, Reece. I just want you to be happy." She smiles at me sadly.

"I'm fine, Chrissy."

A flash of movement catches my eye, and I glance toward the door.

It's Macey. A flicker of an unidentifiable emotion crosses her face as she says, "Sorry, I didn't mean to interrupt. I just wanted to confirm the time for tonight."

I know it's just an excuse because I cleared the time with her upstairs. I'm not sure if she came down here to see me or was merely curious about club business. Her gaze wanders from me over to Chrissy, and she goes completely still.

Chrissy's dressed in her black vintage lingerie—lacy high-waisted panties, garters, stockings with a seam that runs up the back, and on top, a corset that allows her ample breasts to spill over. I'm so accustomed to seeing her like this, I don't even look twice, but Macey's cheeks flush.

"No, I was just leaving," Chrissy says, rising to her feet. "I have to get back to work. I have a bossy Dom who'll be here any minute, and he'll redden my ass if I'm late." She smiles. "Oh, *darn*."

I chuckle as Chrissy heads to the door. She's good at her job, that's for sure.

Chrissy pauses at the door before exiting and faces Macey. "Be careful with him," she says before sauntering away. Macey remains speechless near the door.

"Seven o'clock," I remind Macey. "Wear something nice."

She nods and ducks out of my office, escaping like a scared little mouse.

Well, that was interesting.

• • •

At ten minutes to seven, I walk into the restaurant and request a table in the back. I want to be here when Macey arrives. And after working all afternoon, I need a few minutes to get in the right mind space for this conversation.

Leave it to her to walk back into my life and uproot everything in a matter of two damn days. Christ, I've been letting her walk all over me, call

all the shots. That won't do. I need to regain the upper hand. She hasn't seen my dominant side, but she's about to.

After being seated at the white-clothed table with a small candle in the center, I order us a bottle of wine. The lighting is dim, and all of the other patrons seem to be couples. Frowning down at the candle bathing our secluded table and two wineglasses in a romantic glow of light, I mutter a silent curse. Why had I insisted on bringing Macey here? It feels romantic in a way that this situation doesn't call for. All she's looking to do is forget her troubles for a while, and I'm the man she wants to do it with. I need to treat her as I would any new submissive entering the scene.

Moments later, the hostess escorts a timid-looking Macey back to greet me. I drink in her long glossy hair that I want to wrap in my fist, her tight and curvy body built for a man's pleasure, and that sinful mouth I want to fuck. As beautiful as she is, seeing her reminds me of the past, a painful past that I've tucked away and tried to forget. She was my first love—the girl who broke my heart—and I've changed a lot since then. No sense in reverting now because those big blue eyes are latched onto mine as if she'd follow me anywhere.

I need to remain cool and detached, just like I would with any potential sub, but damn if I don't want to collar her and drag her back to my bed and fuck her senseless.

Rising from the table, I walk slowly and deliberately toward her. Macey's eyes widen and her mouth opens as if she wants to say something, but just as quickly she closes it and lets me take her hand, escorting her away from the hostess and toward our table. Before pulling out her chair, I lean in close and drop my voice to a whisper.

"Tonight, I'm going to treat you as I would any other sub. Which means I'm in charge, and you will do as I ask. Any complaints or issues with that, Pancake?" My voice is calm and steady, and Macey takes note.

She shakes her head, wisely choosing to remain silent. When I pull out her chair, she gracefully lowers herself into her seat, and I can't help but notice how sexy she looks wearing a black minidress and matching six-inch heels. *Damn*. The little girl I once knew has definitely grown up. She's a fucking bombshell.

Before we have the chance to settle in, the waitress approaches the table, looking between us. Her gaze lingers on me long enough that Macey rolls her eyes.

"Are you out for a special occasion?" the waitress asks.

I glance at Macey and fight off a smirk. "You could say that."

"Anything other than the wine, miss?" the waitress asks Macey.

"This is great, thank you." Her eyes lock on me when she answers, as if she's already a sub in my care, looking for guidance and direction. My cock twitches under the table.

"I'll just give you a minute with the menus then," the waitress says, then scampers off.

I pour Macey a glass of red wine and set it in front of her. Her shoulders are stiff, and she's clutching the menu so hard her knuckles are white. Remembering that it's my job to set her at ease, I glance up at her over my menu. "I forgot to ask earlier, how's your nana?"

The mood relaxes instantly, and she smiles up at me. "She's good. She'll be eighty-one this year. Cam and I want to plan her a big party with all of her friends from the retirement community."

"Sounds like fun."

"Oh, you know, tapioca pudding and Polka music. It'll be off the hook."

Her smile is sunny and bright, and I can't help but chuckle at her. She's so strong and well-adjusted, despite losing her parents at such a tender age. It's just one of the many things I admire about Macey.

"Tonight we'll discuss the parameters of your training."

She rolls her eyes. "Yes, my sexless BDSM training. Sounds like a blast."

"That's your brother's request, not mine."

"It's not his business who I let near my vagina, Reece. We both know that. I'm an adult now."

A woman at the neighboring table is staring at us, so I lean closer to Macey. "Keep your voice down," I remind her. "We don't want to attract an audience." I might be good fodder for Chicago's gossip websites, but I'd rather keep my private life private.

She rolls her eyes. "I'm serious about this. I told you what I wanted. You've told me what my brother wants. But what do *you* want?"

I pull a deep breath into my lungs and study the woman seated before me. *What do I want?* That's the million-dollar question.

Ever since Macey so casually strolled out of

my life without so much as a backward glance, things turned to shit. My parents divorced after twenty-three years of marriage, each moving to opposite coasts. My dad is in New Jersey with his brothers and family, while my mom is trying to recapture her youth, living in Redondo Beach and dating a surf instructor.

Meanwhile, I quietly built my business, casually experimenting with submissives to pass the time, never giving thought to what I really want. And now it seems I have the chance to do that. But wanting something and taking what you shouldn't have are two different things. Just because my body wants the physical pleasure that being with Macey would provide, does that make it right? I'm sure Hale won't think so. Maybe I was stupid to ask his permission. Now that I have his parameters, doesn't that make it worse when I take her anyway?

"I promised your brother there wouldn't be any sexual contact in these lessons," I repeat. Maybe if I say it enough times, it'll get easier to swallow, but I doubt it.

"Where's the fun in that?" She's pouting, actually fucking pouting those pretty pink lips at me. Those lips that I've imagined wrapped around my cock since day since she arrived.

I lean closer and tuck a lock of auburn hair behind her ear. "I know, sweetheart, but I'm trying here. I'm trying to instruct you, and also be a good friend to Hale."

"What *Hale* doesn't know won't hurt him. We're both grown-ups, right?"

"Yes."

"Don't your lessons usually involve sex?"

"Yes," I say, unequivocally. *Fuck. Yes.*

"Well, I want my junk touching your junk. Do you want that too?"

"Yeah," I choke out. *Did she just say junk?*

"Okay then, it's settled. Three lessons. Our genitals will be friends, and that's it. At the end of it, we part ways."

That's what I'm afraid of.

I take a deep breath, steeling my resolve. I have to stick to the terms of our agreement—three lessons. Three opportunities to show Macey who's in charge. There can be no emotional ties. No, this will be all about the physical.

Even if my heart wanted her at one time, things have changed. My faith in love has been all but obliterated, initially by my own first love, then by watching my parents' marriage dissolve into a nasty battle. Later it was further damaged by witnessing my best friend's betrayal by the woman he gave his heart to. I've been successful at completely tuning it all out, allowing me to become the man I am today.

The only kind of relationship I want is the kind where naked women trust me with their willing bodies and curious minds. I live for that hazy, disoriented sub-space look in their eyes after a particularly intense scene. The one that tells me they idolize my very existence and will do anything I command. I feel ten feet tall in those moments, like a pure sex god built for doling out pleasure and punishment.

Taking Macey to that place is something I've fantasized about, but never thought I'd make a reality. Do I dare go there with the woman who once owned me so completely?

You bet your sweet ass I'm going to. You only live once, right? There's a saying for this . . . *carpe diem* or something. Seize the day, I think. Macey is giving me her submission on a silver platter, and what happens behind closed doors will be our business. Hale doesn't call all the shots, even if he likes to think he does.

Leaning forward with my elbows on the table, I lift my gaze to Macey's. "What I want, sweetheart is you naked, bound, and spread open before me, your wrists laced together with my rope, your ankles pinned with my spreader bar. Your cunt waiting for me to fill it. You will be used as I see fit. Do you understand?"

Her quick inhalation of breath signals this is an

idea she finds appealing, which only excites me more. I have to remind myself to keep detached.

"Will I be gagged?" she asks.

"No." I smile at her. "You won't be gagged. I'll want to hear all the pretty whimpers and cries falling from your mouth."

"And what about you?" she asks. "Will I be able to touch you? Kiss you?"

My own heart rate spikes despite the calm, cool demeanor I'm struggling to keep in place. "Do you want those things?"

Nodding eagerly, she meets my stare. "I think you know I do."

"I don't know you anymore, Macey. You keep forgetting that. You've walked back in my life like we can pick up right where we left off, but we've both changed."

She watches me for a few quiet moments, as if she wants to disagree. "You never answered the question." A smile twitches on her mouth.

"You will touch me when, how, and where I say." My tone comes out harsher than I intended. *Damn, get it together.* "And kissing is not something I generally do with my submissives, but given our history, I'll take it under advisement."

Fuck, there's nothing I want more than my mouth on hers. Watching her pretty blue eyes fall closed, feeling the warmth of her tongue sweep against mine . . .

I down the remainder of my wine, then catch her gaze. "We need to cover a few things. How many sexual partners have you had?"

She licks her lips, looking down at her plate. I don't know why she's embarrassed to tell me her number. Unless it's really high . . . or really low . . .

"Macey? Look at me."

She clears her throat, and her eyes dart up. "Two."

"That's it?" Fuck me, that's not what I was expecting. It makes me want her pussy on my mouth. Right now.

The waitress saunters up and stops next to our table. "Ready to order?"

Hell yeah, I am. Pussy à la carte, please.

Well aware Macey hasn't absorbed a word of the menu she's been studying, I glance at her. "May I?"

She nods.

"We'll have the coconut chicken with avocado and mango salad, please." It's one of the best things on their menu. "Rice and beans?" I direct my question toward Macey.

"Sure."

"An order of each," I tell the waitress, and we hand over our menus.

"Thank you," Macey says.

I want to thank her for trusting me, but I don't. I simply nod. There's nothing more beautiful than a sub who can feel at ease and confident enough to fully hand me the reins. And something tells me we're well on our way. It makes the Dominant inside me roar to life.

There's a delicate dance happening between us. We know each other intimately, yet we don't. I've changed a lot from the man she remembers. I've grown harder and more distant with every passing relationship that didn't measure up to what she and I once shared. And Macey, I can't even begin to imagine what she's been through, having her heart broken by some MILF-chasing douchebag. Starting over in her hometown after living away for many years.

"It's an interesting scenario . . . you and I . . . our history," I say.

"How so?" she asks, her fingers delicately fingering the stem of her wineglass.

"Generally my first meeting with a new submissive is more question and answer. I'm working to gain her trust, but with you, I sense I already have that."

She levels me with those big blue eyes.

"You've always had it."

"Back then, you and I . . ." I'm searching for the right words and failing. "Things got pretty heated between us . . ."

"You weren't the first."

A wave of possessiveness rushes through me. "I should have been." There's no hesitation, but after I say it, I wish I could take it back. I need to hold my cards closer to the chest, so to speak. I'll give myself away if I'm not careful.

She nods. "In my mind you were."

"What do you mean?" Now I'm intrigued.

"I was with someone who didn't know what he was doing."

"Did you come?"

A short bark of laughter erupts from her. "Not even close."

"That's a damn shame."

"When I think back on that night, in my mind,

we always go all the way."

"Yeah? And how am I?"

"Eh." She smiles that cocky smirk of a smile, the one I want desperately to kiss right off her face.

"Naughty girl." I chuckle at her. Now that the mood's been lightened somewhat, I press on. "Tonight will be about outlining your needs."

She nods.

"You've stated that you're looking to lose yourself. To clear your mind of clutter and enjoy carnal pleasures. In our lessons, my role will be to push you further than you've been before. Your role will be to trust me, and listen to your body."

Nodding again, she takes a thoughtful sip of her wine.

Generally speaking, my role in this sort of meeting is to learn the person, learn her goals, limits, and any weak points she has. Later I will exploit those to the point of discomfort, with the goal of turning them into strengths and make her confidence soar at what she's able to achieve during a session. Damn, if I'm not rock-fucking-hard just thinking about it.

Luckily, the waitress chooses that moment to deliver our meal. I take the opportunity to cool down by serving Macey a piece of chicken from the platter, along with spoonfuls of rice and beans.

"Eat up," I encourage her.

Lifting her fork to her mouth, she's quiet for now, but I can tell her brain is spinning. We enjoy half of our meal that way until my fiery Macey is back.

"Why do you do this?" she finally asks. "Why do you like submissive women?"

"First off, I don't want you to see the word submissive with a negative connotation. It's much more gratifying to watch a strong-willed woman submit to my desires than it is to engage with a doormat who'll go along with anything I say. Don't you think?"

She raises one eyebrow and stabs a slice of mango on her plate. "I suppose."

"Don't confuse this for what it is—I want an equal partner. Just because I'll be the one calling the shots doesn't mean you have no free will. In fact, I quite like spark in my women."

"Does vanilla sex bore you?" she asks.

"No, vanilla sex doesn't bore me. I just haven't had a girlfriend or a serious relationship in a long time. And I tend to reserve that type of close, intimate sex with someone I'm involved with." She doesn't know the half of it.

"Makes sense, I guess," she murmurs.

The wine has gotten to me, or maybe it's just the effect this gorgeous girl has on me. She and I once shared so much.

Time to bring us back to business. "I only have two rules."

She swallows a bite of her food, waiting for me to continue.

"That you use your safe word if things get too intense, and when this is over, it's over. Three lessons, no strings, no attachments. I need you to agree to both rules right now, or the deal's off."

She frowns at the sudden change in my amiable mood. "Geez, so bossy."

"I'm serious, Macey. Things are different this time."

"I see that."

Softening my tone, I add, "Your safety will always be a top priority, both physically and mentally. You don't have to worry about that."

She fiddles with her cloth napkin. "I'd be lying if I didn't admit I'm a little nervous."

"It's good to be nervous. It lets you know where you weak points are. Together, we'll push past your comfort zone until you're in that beautiful oblivion known as sub space."

"What's that?"

"If I do my job correctly, you'll be transported into a trance-like state. It's a euphoric glow, akin to being drunk on wine, I suppose. But what goes up must come down. Just like feeling the effects of a hangover after consuming alcohol, you may feel exhausted, emotional, confused over your role in what just happened, or even physical soreness."

She raises her chin, almost as though she's acknowledging my words as a challenge. "I see."

I pause while the waitress clears our dishes from the table, and when we're alone again, I lean forward and reach under the table. Giving the legs of her chair a tug, I pull her closer. My desire for her has been building all throughout the meal. The need to give her a taste of the fun we'll have together overwhelms me. My hand finds her thigh and skims the hem of her dress.

Macey sucks in a sharp inhale.

Our table in the dimly light restaurant is secluded, but not private, and the secret thrill of being discovered only adds to the sexually intoxicating mood.

Pushing my fingers under her dress, I slide my palm against the bare skin of her thigh. Her skin is silky smooth, and her legs part under my touch.

"Are you sure you're ready for this, Pancake?" I clip out in a low tone.

She makes a small murmuring sound in the back of her throat, signaling to me that she's more than ready for whatever I can dish up.

Jesus. Am I ready for this?

I lean closer across the table and my fingers find her center—and the lacy fabric covering her pussy. As I brush my fingers over her clit, she swears under her breath and grips the edge of the table.

"Has it been a while since a man's properly taken care of you?"

She nods, her chest beginning to show the telltale signs of arousal. She's flushed and pink, and breathing hard already.

Sometimes I still dream about her. Macey was a shy girl but confident with her body, touching her breasts for me while I watched, opening the delicate petals of her pussy to show me her swollen clit. I liked giving orders back then, and she took every one like a personal challenge. Maybe this won't be so different after all. I find the hard nub of her clit and press down, eliciting the most beautiful little whimper from her.

With my free hand, I raise a finger to my lips. "Shh. Quiet."

Macey nods.

As I move my fingers back and forth, Macey's panties grow damp and her breathing is ragged. Just when her thighs begin to tremble, I shove the lace of her panties aside and ever so slowly sink one finger inside her heat. Her tight pussy grips me, sucking at my finger.

My cock is so hard it hurts. I don't know why I insist on torturing myself where Macey's concerned.

"I just remembered. Rule number three. You don't come until I say so."

"Reece," she whimpers.

"You're close, aren't you?" That didn't take long. She's right about one thing. She's wound up tight and in need of relief. And I'll deliver, but not before I demonstrate to her exactly who's running this show.

Whether her eyes are pleading with me to stop or continue, I can't tell. "I'm going to . . . ," she whispers, her voice hoarse.

I pull my hand from beneath the table, and the look painted across her features is pure anguish. She was right there. Right at that beautiful, blissful moment where nothing else exists but blinding pleasure and the building sense of release.

"Not yet. When you come all over my hand, we'll be somewhere private where I can enjoy every second of it."

"Then why the hell did you do that?" she asks,

breathless and clearly frustrated.

I shrug, my mouth turning up in a smirk. "Just wanted to see if I could still get you off in under a few minutes."

She frowns. "Well, don't you deserve a pat on the back? Are we done here?"

"Eager," I remark. Her pussy juices are drying on my finger, and it takes all my restraint not to bring my hand to my mouth to taste her. I'm a caveman, but I still have *some* impulse control. "Yes, let's go."

I leave a wad of cash on the table, including a generous tip for our waitress. I've never fingered a submissive under the table before, but something tells me our little show might not have gone as undetected as I thought. The waitress and busboy are grinning at me like we're sharing a private secret. *Great.* That better not be in the headlines tomorrow.

I escort Macey back to my apartment, both of us quiet on the walk.

When we reach the club, Crave is in full swing, and I keep my hand at Macey's lower back as we maneuver our way through the crowded club. Sex and money are in the air, and normally I'd feel jovial, and probably sit down at the bar for a while to see if anyone interesting caught my eye. Tonight, I shoot scowls at the men openly admiring Macey. I can't wait to get upstairs. And lock the goddamn door.

When we get inside, I turn on the lights and head for the kitchen. "I'm going to get a Scotch," I call over my shoulder. "Would you like one?"

Macey slams the door.

What the hell? "Is that a no to the Scotch, sweetheart?"

"Are you serious right now?" She storms into the kitchen and squares off with me, anger slashed across her pretty features.

"About?"

"That's it? The night's over?"

I swallow to avoid revealing the smile playing at my lips. She's angry about earlier and wants to continue playing. *Perfect.*

Taking a step closer, I pin her with my gaze. "I'm not your boyfriend, and I'm not your fuck friend. I'm your Dom. We'll play on my terms, in a private room I'll reserve for us in my club. Not before then. Do you understand me?" I finish pouring my measure of Scotch and wait.

She huffs out a frustrated breath. I think she's going to argue, but instead she stomps from the kitchen, calling out an exaggerated, "Fine," over her shoulder. When she heads straight for my bedroom, curiosity takes over and I immediately follow.

"What do you think you're doing?" I find her in my closet, down on her knees and rummaging through a black duffel bag that just happens to hold all my sex toys. Apparently she did see this when she cleaned up.

"Ah, here we go." Her fingers close around a generously sized flesh-colored vibrating dildo.

"You won't do the job? Well, I have a feeling this baby will." She waves it in the air like she's found the damn golden ticket. Then she rises to her feet and smiles sweetly at me.

For the love of God, this woman does not fight fair. She never has. "Where do you think you're going with that?"

"Probably my bed, then the shower." A line creases her forehead. "Do you have spare batteries for this thing? It might be a *long* night."

"No way. Not happening. Give me the toy, Macey." I reach out a hand, my voice as stern as the set of my jaw, my fingers barely avoiding crushing the crystal tumbler in my other hand.

A slow smile uncurls on her mouth. "Why, Reece Jackson, are you jealous?" She eyes the toy in her hand and then lets her gaze slip seductively down to the crotch of my pants.

If she really thinks that toy's size has me feeling insecure, she's insane. Certifiably. "You really don't remember, do you?" Now I'm the one smiling. She'll be in for a pleasant surprise later.

"I remember everything. I remember how you always made me keep my underwear on, and that I never actually saw you"—her gaze flicks downward—"down there. I only felt you with my hand, and since I had nothing to base it on, I assumed all guys were like that."

"Well, in that case, you'll be sorely disappointed with this toy." I snatch the dildo from her hand and toss it back in the open bag.

"What do you think you're doing?" she asks, planting a hand on her hip. "You left me hanging at the restaurant."

"And you will stay like that until I say so."

"You can't be serious. I'm not allowed to masturbate?"

I shake my head. Unless she wants to perform a private show for me, no. "No touching yourself, no toys, and definitely no other men, until I say." I take her hand. "Come on, I'll show you how to drink

Scotch."

"Reece, stop." Her voice makes me pause on my way from the closet.

I face her and place my finger against her plump lower lip. "You're trying to top from the bottom, and the more you fight this, the longer it'll take. Give up control. Go with it, okay?"

I'm not going to explain every small detail to her. Now that we covered how this works, I need some time to properly set up a scene. I won't rush this. I've been waiting six years.

"Fine," she says, her voice small.

She follows me into the living room and we sit down on the sofa, side by side. It's not lost on me that we're alone in my apartment. We could be fucking each other's brains out right now. I have a drawer full of condoms, and God knows, she's willing.

But I know myself better now than I did six years ago. I need to keep the control in this situation, separate the sex from the emotion. And the only way I know to do that is through carefully crafting a scene and performing within its parameters. And that takes planning and preparation.

I wanted to give her the world at one time, and I would have. Now I'm questioning my decision to share three sessions with her.

"Good things come to little girls who wait," I murmur, tucking a stray lock of chestnut-colored hair behind her ear.

"You're a confusing man," she says, blinking those stunning baby blues up at me.

"For good reason, my pet. Trust me."

"I do," she says without hesitation.

Ignoring the little pang I feel in my chest, I continue. "Now, I know you drink whiskey, but what about Scotch?"

"What's the difference?" she asks, leaning closer and watching me swirl the amber-colored liquor in my glass.

"I'll show you. Drinking Scotch is like having a one-night stand with a grizzly bear. If you're not careful, you'll regret it in the morning."

She glares at me, not amused, probably still cranky from the orgasm-denial tactic I used with her earlier. *Too fucking bad. I didn't get off either, princess.*

"And for another thing," I continue. "Scotch is whiskey made in Scotland and aged in oak barrels for at least three years."

She raises an eyebrow.

"Close your eyes."

"Stop being ridiculous. A little bit of Scotch isn't going to douse this need I have."

"The sooner you cooperate, the sooner—"

"Fine." She closes her eyes and fixes a polite smile on her face. "Happy?"

"For now." I bring the glass under her nose.

"Inhale." She does, drawing a deep breath, and with it the distinct harsh scent. "Good. Open your eyes."

She does, blinking them at me, clearly wondering what game we're playing.

"Scotch is a man's drink. The taste is raw masculinity filled with complex, biting flavors, a rich caramel color, and even a price tag that speaks of sophistication and dominance."

"I see," she says, her response coming out as more of an exhale than actual words.

"Scotch is a drink that's meant to be savored and enjoyed slowly. Just like my first time with a new submissive, it's important to use care and go slowly. Tossing it back as a shot would be a damn shame for something so exquisite."

Her eyes follow mine as understanding dawns in them. I'm not in this for a quick fuck. We will do this, explore this thing between us, but it will be in a controlled fashion, and it'll happen when and how I say.

"Open for me." I bring the glass to her mouth

and allow her a tiny sip, knowing the smoky flavors are burning her tongue as she swallows.

Everything I do, the core of who I am now, is all about restraint. I don't know why it's so important for me that she see that. It just is. I'm not that carefree, hope-filled guy of twenty she remembers. From the way I conduct my business to the scenes I share with my subs, it's a transaction. A give and take. Goal. Set. Match.

"Reece?" She averts her eyes, her fingers toying with the hem of her dress in the most distracting way.

"Hmm?"

"Can I ask you something?"

"Of course you can."

"Will you be . . . are you . . ."

"Get it out, sweetheart."

"Are you sleeping with anyone else?"

Straightening my shoulders, I set the glass of

Scotch on the low table in front of us. "I don't see how that's any of your business." My tone is gruff and I instantly regret it. I hate how all my reactions with her make me feel as if I've done something wrong.

My rough growl is like a slap. She lowers her chin to her chest and twists her hands in her lap. "Well, I just wanted to tell you that I'm not, and I'm clean. I got tested after I found out Tony was cheating on me."

Shit. Now I feel like even more of an asshole. She's trying to have a serious, adult conversation with me, and I respond with some possessive, macho comment.

Lifting her chin, I force her gaze to mine. "That's good to know. I don't have anyone else I'm seeing right now, and I'm clean too. But whenever we play, we can use condoms if you prefer."

A small smile forms on her lips. "No," she murmurs. "If it's just me and you, we don't have to."

Fucking hell. The erection I was sporting all throughout dinner? That motherfucker is back, pressing on my zipper and throbbing like it's his damn job. Knowing I'll be balls deep inside her without a layer of latex between us is ... indescribable.

Macey rises from the couch. "I better get some sleep. I'm meeting Cameron's new fiancée tomorrow."

Shit, that's right. Hale proposed, and Brielle said yes. "You'll like Brielle. She's sweet, and she's good for him." I rise to my feet and Macey gives me a hug to thank me for dinner. "How long until your new place is ready?"

"Not long. Is that a problem?"

"You can stay as long as you like. I'm just trying to figure out if I should have you a key made."

"No, I'll be out of your hair in a few days."

I nod, ignoring the deeper meaning behind her

words, and the sinking feeling in the pit of my gut. "Good night."

Chapter Six

Macey

Of course I'm running late. Today will be my first time meeting Brielle, the new woman in my brother's life. From the little bits I've picked up through conversations with Reece and Cameron, I sense that this is something he's serious about, which surprises me given his past.

After the fiasco with his ex, that bitch-face Tara, I watched my brother change into a man I barely recognized. He grew hard, cold, and distant. I knew he was spending a lot of time with Reece, and now I understand why. He was sinking deep into the world of BDSM, a world I don't understand, but I aim to. A world with mystery and sex and possibilities. It's not lost on me that the exact thing Cameron ran to after licking his wounds is the same thing I'm doing post-breakup. *Maybe it runs in the family.*

Locating a parking spot at the restaurant/wine bar where we're meeting, I maneuver my car into the tight space and kill the engine. This next hour should be nothing if not interesting.

As I make my way inside, I smooth my silk top over my hips, which seem to have grown rounder. Unless these jeans shrank. *Geez*. Refusing to feel self-conscious, I brush the thought away. That dipshit Tony would have slept with Pinky regardless of what I looked like, I'm pretty sure. Besides, Reece seemed to have no problem with my appearance. The way his dark brown eyes caressed every curve, every detail made me feel flushed and warm. I've filled out from the girl of eighteen he once knew.

Entering the restaurant, I pause to allow my eyes a moment to adjust to the dim interior. We're meeting at a new wine bar in the heart of Chicago, and despite it being a little early in the afternoon for happy hour, there are couples and a few small groups seated at the bar and high-top tables filling the space.

I spot Cameron immediately. He sees me too, rising to his feet with a warm smile to greet me.

"You found it," he says, putting his arm around me for a hug.

Despite not living here for the last several years, my brain seems to recall the city. "Your directions were perfect. Good to see you." I return his hug.

The woman with him rises to her feet too. She's petite and pretty, with wide eyes and a pouty mouth. It's clear why he likes her. But when I notice her hair is in a casual ponytail and she's dressed simply—wearing jeans, flats, and a plain cotton sweater—I decide I like her too. At first glance, she's nothing like the overdone designer-wearing, fully manicured ex I despise. That's an automatic ten points right there.

"Macey, I'd like you to meet Brielle."

"Hello," she says, softly, looking between Cameron and me as if she's nervous.

I suppose this is akin to meeting his family, because with our parents gone, it's only me. Well, and Nana.

"It's great to finally meet you," I say, leaning toward her with open arms for a hug.

She squeezes me and then we each take a step back, and when we do, we're both smiling.

Cameron watches us, his contemplative mood hard to read. He's quiet, and whenever his gaze flicks over to me, he frowns.

The waitress strolls up, delivering the drink menu.

"Shall I pick us a bottle?" Cameron asks us, glancing at the selection.

"Sure," Brielle and I both say at the same time.

Trying to keep the mood light and friendly, I ask Brielle about her work and where she grew up, and she chats steadily as we sip our wine. My first hunch was correct—I like her. She's sweet and smart, obviously a nice, normal girl, which is all

I've ever wanted for my brother.

Cameron is so quiet, I ask him what's wrong, but he merely shakes his head, frowning at me again. *What the hell crawled up his ass?* It's the first time I've seen him since Reece spoke with him about our arrangement. I guess he's not as okay with it as I thought.

When he excuses himself for the men's room, I use the opportunity to switch to some girl talk, and maybe even pump Brielle for information.

"Well, everything I heard from Reece and Cam about you has been spot-on. I can tell you're going to be really good for my brother."

She smiles at me. "Thank you. He's an amazing man, and I'm lucky to have him in my life." We smile at each other for a sappy moment, before she asks, "You know Reece?"

"Yes. He and I have an interesting past. I had no idea about this current . . . preferences, though."

"He's a fascinating guy, that's for sure," she

says, her cheeks flushing slightly.

"So I take it you know about the club." God, I hate to think about her and my brother there. *Ew. Gag me.*

Brielle's eyes widen and she chokes on her sip of wine. "Uh . . ."

Knitting my brows in confusion, I really hope I'm not stuffing my foot in my mouth. "I'm sorry . . . I thought . . ."

"Yes, I do," she answers definitively.

"What can you tell me about Reece's involvement in BDSM?" I hate that I suddenly feel like a lawyer, interrogating her for information. In my mind, this was going to be a smoother conversation. Instead I'm blurting things out without even thinking.

"I can't speak much to that. I can only speak to what I've seen of him, and from what Hale has told me. Reece is a good man, but he's doesn't trust women. Hale says he should've taken a sub years ago, but he's stubborn and refuses to settle down."

Interesting.

"Why? Are you . . ." Brielle squints at me, apparently trying to read my intentions.

I shrug. "I'm just coming off of a bad breakup and looking to have some fun, that's all." I hold up my hands in surrender. "And Crave seems like the perfect place to do it."

"A rebound fling," she says. Frowning, she swirls the wine in her glass. "Just be careful with him. Reece is one of the good guys. I wouldn't want to see him get hurt."

Her concern feels genuine, but it's misplaced. I'm pretty sure the big, bad Dom can handle himself. But before I can answer, Brielle's eyes widen, and I sense Cameron's presence looming behind me. I turn and see him fuming, his jaw ticking

"For fuck's sake. First Reece comes to me, and now this." Cameron pulls out his chair, but he doesn't sit. He remains standing over me. "Listen up, Macey. You're my goddamn sister. I don't want to hear about your exploits. I don't want to think about you getting in over your head with this. Lucky for you, I trust Reece implicitly. But I still don't want it thrown in my face."

Letting out a deep sigh, I fight against the anger rising inside me. He has no place telling me who or what I can do. "I didn't like learning about your involvement in the club either." I nod to Brielle. "I don't like thinking about you tying up your fiancée here in knots and doing God knows what, so let's just agree to one thing right now. You stay out of my sex life and I'll steer clear of yours. Deal?"

Shoving his hands in his pockets, he frowns and glares at me, obviously fighting to maintain his composure. "Done."

I'm pretty sure he wants to punch something, but at least he's going to back off. For now, anyway.

I toss back the last swig of my wine. "I think I better be going. It was very nice meeting you,

Brielle. I'm sorry things got a little awkward at the end." I try to chuckle, but it feels weird on my lips, and Brielle looks at me with sympathy. *Hell.*

"No, it's not awkward at all. I'm so happy we met." She pulls her cell phone from her purse, insisting that we swap numbers. "If you need anything as you get settled back into the city, anything at all, please call me. Even if it's just to go get a pedicure, or someone to drink a margarita with."

I fight back a strange wave of emotion at Brielle's offer. I really don't have any friends left in the city. I'm sure I could look up some old high school friends, but that holds no appeal. High school was a weird time for me. Between losing my parents, being taken in by Nana, and secretly dating Reece, my plate was full, and I just sort of drifted through those couple of years until I could escape.

"Thank you. I will," I promise. "I love a good margarita."

"I know just the place then. Text me whenever." She stands up and hugs me.

I seriously love this girl.

"Good job with this one," I tell Cameron, some of my annoyance toward him fading.

"Thanks, sis. I love you, you know."

"Yeah, I know." I pull on my coat and grab my wallet. "Can I chip in for the wine?"

He shakes his head. "I've got it."

I'm guessing they're going to stay and finish the rest of the bottle, and he's being kind—he knows I don't have a job yet. My savings was padded pretty nicely, but still, that won't last me forever.

"See you around!" I call out over my shoulder, stealing one last look at the cute couple.

I used to be that couple, in love with wide-eyed happiness. Now I'm a jaded, unemployed hot mess. I head back to Crave, which seems to be quickly becoming my own little escape from reality.

Chapter Seven

Reece

I'm talking with my security manager in the camera room when Macey arrives back at the club. I watch her walk through the bar on the screen overhead. She moves confidently toward the elevator, looking sexy, her hips swaying as she walks. I can't help but remember last night on the couch, feeding her small sips of Scotch as I watched her body's reactions to me and the liquor, the way her nipples hardened beneath her dress, begging to be licked.

"Boss?" he asks.

"What?" *What the fuck were we talking about?*

It's crazy how just the sight of her gets my blood pumping, my dick hard, and all thoughts to flee my brain, only to be replaced with fantasies of pinning her down and fucking her hard and fast.

"That switch who lost her paddle last weekend . . . what do you want me to do?"

Oh, right. "We're not a fucking lost and found. Tell her it's her responsibility to keep track of her equipment while she's here. End of fucking story. Now, are we done here?"

He nods sharply. "Yes. Got it."

"Good."

I stride from the office and head straight toward the elevator, still able to pick up notes of Macey's scent in the air. After checking in with my staff, I planned to go back to my office and get a few more hours of work done, but now nothing can keep me from jumping into what I know will probably end in a big fucking mess.

The elevator takes its sweet-ass time, but finally I stroll into my apartment. "Macey?" I call out, not seeing her.

Music comes from the guest room, so I knock lightly on the door.

She opens it, looking good enough to eat. Her hair flows in loose waves over her shoulders, and her big blue eyes latch onto mine. She's dressed in fitted jeans that hug her spankable ass, and a silk top that drapes beautifully over her full breasts. Her skin looks so soft, I want to reach out and touch it, just to prove to myself that there's no way it's as soft as I remember.

"Busy?"

She glances back to the laptop that's open on her bed. "No, I was just shopping for curtains online."

I tilt my head, continuing to watch her. "Would you like to do something more interesting?"

"Sure." She smiles at me, her brain already working.

I lean in close, letting my mouth and nose brush over her neck, and feel the pulse thrumming under her skin. She smells incredible, lightly scented with lavender and vanilla. I want to taste her, but that will come later when she's naked and waiting, and I can take my time licking from one spot to the next.

"You are to go down to the third floor and meet me in my private play room. It's the last room on the end, and the security code is 0413."

"Your birthday," she says without hesitation.

Pausing, I swallow, surprised as hell that she remembers that detail. "Yes. April thirteenth."

She looks down at her outfit. "Should I get ready first?"

Fighting off a smile, I shake my head. She'll be in her birthday suit soon. "You're fine like that. Let yourself into the room, and remove your shirt and jeans. I want you to wait for me on the bed in your bra and panties. While you wait, think of your safe word. When I arrive, you'll tell me what it is."

"Okay," she says softly. A pink flush spreads over her chest, as if she's realizing this is really about to happen.

My own heart is hammering in my chest as I watch her turn and head for the door. Her round, apple-shaped ass taunts me with every step she takes. I can feel myself slipping already, and we haven't even begun.

When the door to the apartment closes, followed shortly by the ding of the elevator, I dig my cell phone out of my pocket and press the button for a number I haven't called in a long time.

"Oliver?"

"Hey, Reece. How are things?"

"I need some backup in a scene. Are you free?"

"Sure. Not a problem. When are you thinking?"

"Give me ten minutes, then meet me in my private room."

"See you then."

Arriving at my private room, I pause at the door to type in the security code, then let myself in. The overheard lights are off, and the shades are drawn, leaving only faint splashes of afternoon light to peek around the edges, casting the room in dim shadows. Macey is sitting at the end of the bed, her feet dangling from the floor. The generous swell of her cleavage spills over the cups of her black bra, and a small piece of matching black lace barely covers her between her legs. Her hair is loose, cascading over her bare shoulders, and her cheeks are rosy. She looks perfect.

I stalk closer, moving slowly and deliberately, letting her experience every bit of the uncertainty evident in her features. She chews on her lower lip, waiting, watching me. I stop directly before her, close enough to touch, but for now I keep my hands to myself. My cock is already half-hard, and if she hasn't noticed yet, she's going too soon.

"Have you chosen a safe word?"

"Yes," she says. "Pancake."

I smirk, fighting the urge to bite my lip. "Fine."

Closing her eyes, she shakes her head and draws in a big inhale. "Sorry, I'm just a little nervous."

"About what?" I ask, needing to be further inside her head.

Her gaze drifts to the toy bag I've placed just inside the door. "Pain."

I shake my head. "Nothing to worry about." Something tells me that any scars after our encounters will be psychological, not physical. Besides, I don't enjoy doling out pain. "Can I make you more comfortable?" I ask, my gaze drifting down to the cups of her bra.

She nods.

Reaching behind her, I unclasp her bra, needing her to feel every bit as exposed as I do.

Macey doesn't cover herself; she doesn't cower. She holds her shoulders steady and lets me carefully remove the piece of lacy lingerie.

Her full breasts, unrestricted by the black lace, tumble freely into my waiting hands. It's been years, six torturous years since I could touch her like this and make her feel good. I skim my thumbs across her nipples and she shudders, arching into my touch. Watching her nipples tighten as I stroke them, I'm reminded of little pink gumdrops, my favorite candy, and I bet she tastes just as sweet.

"You have beautiful tits, sweetheart," I tell her.

Macey looks up, continuing to sit perched on the bed while I stroke her breasts and nipples. She presses her thighs together—the movement subtle, but not unnoticed.

"Are those panties getting wet for me already?"

"Yes, sir," she murmurs, pushing her breasts into my hands, letting me massage and fondle her delicate skin. A knock at the door interrupts us, and her half-lidded eyes fly open, her expression puzzled. "Expecting someone?"

"Yes. Sit tight."

I answer the door and let Oliver inside. Part of me is beginning to understand why Hale called me in for backup in his session with Brielle—he might not have known how to handle the depth of his emotional connection to the submissive under his command. No way in hell do I want to explore the similarities there between us.

"Thanks for coming," I say, shaking his hand.

"Of course. However I can help, I'm here."

I turn toward Macey to find she's crossed her arms over her chest, hiding her breasts, and is sitting straight as a stick on the bed like someone jammed a pole up her ass. *Remember when I said I'd be calling the shots, princess?*

I stop in the center of the room, and Oliver stills next to me. "Macey, come here."

Keeping one arm over her chest to cover herself, she slides down off the bed until her feet touch the floor. With her tits jiggling as she moves toward us, Macey's wide gaze pings between me, Oliver, and the floor.

"Remove your hands, please," I say when she's standing directly in front of us.

Her eyes round even more. "Reece?"

"Don't tell me you're going to use that safe word already, and over such a simple request. Show him those gorgeous tits."

She swallows, her nerves evident, though her gaze never wavers from mine. Her lips tighten as she lowers her hands to her side, leaving her in just the black lacy panties that I'm itching to tear from her body. Her stomach is flat, but soft, and her hips curve in that delicious hourglass shape I love on a woman. She looks damn good topless.

I glance at Oliver to see his throat work as he swallows, but ever the consummate Dominant, he appears relaxed, and of course says nothing.

Just as I sense her nerves and confusion peak, I introduce him at last. "This is Oliver. He'll be assisting with your training today."

"Um . . ." Macey shifts her weight from one foot to the other.

"Oliver, this is Macey." I nod to the half-naked beauty in our presence.

He extends his hand toward her and she reaches

out dutifully and shakes it, but I can tell her head is spinning. She's never normally this quiet.

"It's nice to meet you, Macey," Oliver says. "I work here at Crave, teaching classes to couples who are interested in exploring BDSM."

I know she assumed it would just be the two of us—hell, I did too—but at the last minute, I decided to mix it up.

Her eyes find mine, and when I give her a tight nod, she says, "Okay."

Oliver chuckles, his face brightening as he does. "It's okay to feel nervous. Most people do their first time."

"I'm not nervous," she lies.

"Good then. We'll jump right in," I say.

Turning to address Oliver, I palm one of Macey's weighty breasts in my hand. "She's beautiful, isn't she?"

He knows I'm giving him an open initiation to

touch her, but Macey doesn't. It's like Dom code for, *Yes, you can play with my new toy.* I have to do this, I tell myself. She's not mine, and she never will be.

Oliver lifts his hand to her other breast, brushing the back of his knuckles over the generous curve of it, and I instantly want to beat him within an inch of his life. *The cocksucker.* I take a deep breath and reach for my control.

"She's perfect," Oliver says, his tone low. Macey watches me while he strokes her, and I have to tamp down the murderous feelings raging inside me. "Are these C's?" he asks, his voice slightly husky.

"D's," she corrects him, her voice small.

"And real," he adds, feeling the weight of her soft breast in his hand. He plucks her nipple firmly between his thumb and middle finger, and Macey lets out a swift grunt of surprise. "Is ménage one of your hard limits?" Oliver smiles at her sweetly, continuing to caress her breast.

Macey's eyes widen and she opens her mouth, but nothing comes out.

"We'll get to all that later," I say, answering for her. Or maybe I just don't want to hear her answer. "Just some simple play to start first. Macey's a virgin to all this."

Oliver nods, then steps away to retrieve my toy bag.

I take Macey's hand and lead her to the bed. "You okay so far?"

She nods. "Yes."

At my request, she lays down in the center of the bed, leaving Oliver and me free to sit on either side of her on the oversized mattress. As I slide her panties down her legs and drop them from the end of the bed, Oliver sets an arrangement of implements on the bed beside me. They're all harmless, but that doesn't mean Macey's eyes haven't gone as wide as saucers.

"Let's begin with this," I say, picking up a strip

of black silk.

"A blindfold," she says.

"Yes. And while normally I don't permit my subs to speak during a scene unless I ask a question or they need to use their safe word, for this first time, I'll allow it."

She nods.

I hand the blindfold to Oliver and he secures it over her eyes, knotting it behind her head.

"Lay back, and try to relax," I tell her. "Take in all the surroundings, everything you can feel, using all of your senses. Sight often prevents us from seeing things as they truly are. You saw all of my toys, and began to feel anxious."

Then I pick up a large black feather made of synthetic silk and trail it over her belly. "When you're less worried about watching, you're free to actually feel." She begins to relax into the bed as I tickle the feather over her ribs, up to her breasts, and back down again.

Her harsh breathing begins to slow as I treat her to light, soft caresses. "How does this feel?"

Her mouth relaxes, and I can tell she's stopped thinking so much. "It's nice," she murmurs.

I stop at her mound. "Open your legs, sweetheart." She parts her legs, but only a couple of inches. "Nice and wide so Oliver and I can see how pretty and wet your cunt is going to get for us."

She licks her lips and spreads her legs. It's seems she's channeled her inner seductress and is willing to play the game.

"Pretty girl," I murmur, my voice coming out thick. Using my thumbs, I part her inner petals and use the glistening moisture there to stroke her clit.

Macey twists on the bed, lifting her hips toward my hand. Christ, she's been right on the edge since the restaurant. She's going to go off like a rocket, and when she does, I want to be the only man watching her.

My eyes travel up to Oliver's, who's practically

salivating with the desire to taste her sweet juices. When I catch his attention, I mouth silently, *Get the fuck out*, and cut my eyes to the door.

He frowns, his jaw tightening, but rises silently from the bed and crosses the room to leave. There's no sound when the door closes behind him, and I'm certain Macey has no idea he's left.

Grasping my hand that's now resting on her thigh, Macey pulls it back to the juncture between her thighs. "You can touch me, sir," she breathes.

Goddamn it. She's the worst submissive ever.

"I'm going to punish you for that." I ought to spank her. Instead I'm just going to make her suck on my cock and withhold her orgasm until she's ready to cry from frustration.

Removing black leather straps from my bag, I grab each of Macey's ankles, securing them in turn to the bedposts. Then I tie her wrists in front of her in a series of complicated knots that still allow her some movement. She wiggles her fingers and twists on the bed, turning her head from side to side although the blindfold ensures she sees nothing.

"Stay still," I remind her.

Testing her new restraints, she shifts her legs, which remain spread, and moves her hands, which remain tied in front of her. She looks gorgeous naked, bound, and blindfolded. Maybe now she'll be obedient enough to lose herself in this scene.

I tug down my zipper and take out my cock. It's hard, ready, and aching for her touch. Kneeling beside her on the bed, I stroke myself slowly.

"Remember when you asked if you would be able to touch me?"

She turns her face toward my voice. "Yes."

"You're going to make me come, and you're going to do it as quickly as you can. I'm going to time you. However many minutes this takes is how many times I'll spank you when we're done, understand?"

"Yes, sir," she says, a slight tremor to her voice.

"And considering that I can usually fuck for over an hour, you'd better bring your A game."

She sucks in an inhale, her chest shuddering with the movement.

"You want to challenge me? Fine. Here's your chance to take control and test my stamina." I push my hips closer to her until my cock brushes against her bound hands. "Clock's ticking, sweetheart."

Realizing I'm not going to untie her, Macey grips me, awkwardly at first since she can't see what she's doing, and begins stroking up and down. Every time her fist reaches the base, I can feel the brush of the rope against me, and while it's an erotic sight watching her bound hands work up and down against me, it's not exactly the most practical.

"Easy. I don't want rope burn on my dick, baby." Taking her hands, I reposition them, lifting both hands over my shaft so she can use her palms together.

It feels good, even with her clumsy movements, and I'm just about to pat myself on the back for dreaming up this scene when she totally surprises me.

"Can I use my mouth, please, sir?"

Who am I to refuse a request like that? "Permission granted."

Lifting her up by shoulders, I ease her into a sitting position while I continue kneeling before her. I grip my cock at the base and curl one hand around the back of her neck, drawing her forward. "I'm right here."

Unaccustomed to being without her sense of vision, Macey opens her mouth and waits, letting me place the head of my cock on her tongue.

Without hesitating, she slides her mouth down my steely shaft, sucking me in like a motherfucking Hoover vacuum. *What the hell? When did this woman learn how to deep throat like a porn star?*

I fist my hands at my sides, fighting the urge to touch her while she bobs up and down over me, laving her tongue over my shaft and balls, and sucking me down her throat.

Fuck.

Just when I think it can't get any hotter, she lowers her bound hands to her pussy and begins rubbing her clit with one extended finger. My cock hardens even more, my balls drawing up close to my body as my release builds.

I'm a sick fuck, but I can't resist watching this again. The memory of her touching herself back then, working her swollen clit with the pad of her middle finger, just like I showed her, was hypnotic. After, of course I felt like the world's biggest fuck up. I met Hale for a game of basketball later that day, and all I could think about was that I just taught his little sister to masturbate.

Her hot, wet mouth works me over while she brings herself closer and closer to release. I'm transfixed . . . a man out of control. My eyes follow her every greedy movement as she sucks on my cock like it's her favorite candy, and her fingers work faster and faster between her thighs. She whimpers, and moans around me. She's close, and I'm powerless to stop this. Letting out a low, throaty cry, she comes—hard—her thighs trembling, and her mouth continuing to slide up and down on me.

Unable to hold back, I curl one hand around the back of her neck, pushing myself deeper into her mouth as hot jets of semen pulse from deep within me. The power of the release is unexpected, and normally a silent type, I'm surprised to hear the deep groan that rumbles in my chest, and the sound of her name falling from my lips.

Still blindfolded, and bound, Macey sits mute before me. I tug off her blindfold, and work at untying her wrists, checking to be sure they're no lasting marks on her wrists.

"How'd I do?" she asks, a smirk tugging up her well-used mouth.

Glancing at my watch, I'm shocked to see it's only been six minutes. *Six*. That can't be right. I bring the thing to my ear to make sure it's still ticking. *Huh. Son of a bitch.*

Knowing she's fought hard and won back some of the control I took from her, she smiles. I can't enjoy her victory, though, because I feel conflicted and confused in a way that I haven't before following a session. Her smiles falls and she glances around the room.

"Where's Oliver?"

"He left. A while ago actually."

She grins again. "Because you wanted me all to yourself?"

Yes. "No. Because I didn't want him to watch you suck my cock."

"Oh." That pretty face is twisted in confusion again.

"Bend over. Place your cheek on the bed, and present your ass to me."

"Because you're going to spank me?" she asks.

"Six times," I confirm, trying to find that

businesslike persona I generally assume when teaching a new submissive. But Macey is no submissive, and damn if I don't love her spark.

Macey gets into position, laying down on the bed so that her cheek is resting on the soft duvet, her knees are bent under her, and her ass is displayed beautifully for me.

"You have a beautiful ass," I murmur, stroking my thumb over the rosy pink opening. I need to fuck this virgin ass. *Soon.*

"Thank you, sir."

Dammit. I'm hard again. Even after my intense release, I'm aching and ready for her. I hate that she has such a powerful impact on me.

Macey relaxes, letting me caress the perfectly rounded globes of her ass, and stroke the forbidden place I want to make mine with tender touches meant to ease her into the idea.

She moans, just a tiny sound, in her throat, but it tells me she's not entirely opposed to this idea.

With one hand still touching her gorgeous ass, my free hand reaches over to grab my short-tailed flogger, but it feels too stiff and unrelenting in my hand. Strange. It's normally my go-to toy. Opting to use my bare hand instead, I give her a sharp swat against one fleshy ass cheek. Macey inhales sharply. My handprint on her skin turns pink as the blood rushes to the surface, heightening her experience.

Spanking her twice more in quick succession, Macey flinches, and then groans. It's the small sound I needed to hear to know she's not completely hating this.

I soothe her tender skin, running my hand lightly over the surface, my cock is eager, and straining for her, and if I don't finish this soon, I'm going to fuck her right here, and break every rule I have for myself in the process.

Treating her other ass cheek to the same process—I spank her three times in quick succession, and then rise from the bed. The need to get away from here – to distance myself from her flares up inside of me.

"Take as long as you need. There's a soaking tub in the bathroom if you're interested."

I pull on my jeans, and shrug on my T-shirt as I head for the door.

"That's it?" Macey calls behind me.

A sour pit turns in my stomach as the inner turmoil rages inside me. I turn and see her rise up onto her knees on the bed, staring at me with a crease between her brows, and a tight-lipped frown.

Normally, there would be aftercare—cuddling, discussion over the session, maybe even sex, but that's not something I can do with her. Intimacy can't be part of this agreement, and so aftercare isn't an option.

"Did you expect something different?" I ask, making sure to keep my tone neutral. She can't know all the ways she affects me.

But fuck, I can read the hurt and confusion written across her features, and it almost guts me. "I thought . . ." Her voice is shaky, and she doesn't continue.

I nod once, and continue to the door. I'll gather up my toys and clean up the room later. I just need to get back to my apartment, wash the lavender scent of her off my skin and pour myself a large Scotch. Then maybe, just maybe, I can get my head straight. She came here wanting to fuck a Dom – not to rekindle our young love.

Closing the door behind me, old feelings of loss and fear rise up inside me. I've been trying to remain detached, to forget, if only for a brief time the history we share. Well, that was a fucking fail, because as soon as I got Macey inside that private room, all my careful plans fell to shit. Even having Oliver there didn't help. It didn't soften the connection I felt with her, didn't hinder me from feeling that it was just her and I, Dominant and submissive experiencing the most beautiful thing together.

And then she got her mouth on me, and I came faster than a high school band geek. But really, I can't blame myself. Watching her touch her sweet pussy pushed me over the edge. I never gave her permission to touch herself, but then again, I never expressly forbid it either. And damn if I didn't love watching it.

I need to get my fucking shit together, or there won't be a next time.

Chapter Eight

Reece

"What's for dinner, honey?" Hale asks, letting himself into my place.

I'm sitting in my favorite leather armchair in the living room with my feet propped up on the ottoman. Hale said he was stopping by tonight, but I didn't know he'd expect dinner.

"Scotch and M&Ms. Is that cool?" I say, popping another of the colorful candies into my mouth. I have no idea why I thought it was a good idea to buy so much candy last Halloween. A BDSM club gets very few trick-or-treaters, it turns out.

Hale ignores my sarcasm and walks to my bar to pour himself a drink before sinking onto the couch across from me. Once settled, he cocks an eyebrow at me. "Bad day?"

"Something like that." Macey moved to her

apartment today, and when I offered to help, she said that between her brother and Brielle and Brielle's friend Kirby, they had it covered.

So I sat here and sulked like an asshole all day. I never expected her to stay, but the way she left— so abruptly, so easily, refusing my offer for help without even a backward glance—something about it set me off. The damn woman is independent to her core, and it drives me crazy. I planned to hit the gym and catch up on some work, but I felt unmotivated to do either.

Glancing down at the candies on the table, Hale frowns at me. "Seriously, dude? This is your dinner?"

"Yeah, why?"

"Because we're not thirteen anymore." He pauses to pick up a piece of candy from the table, looking at it thoughtfully. "Brielle cooks. She makes sure I eat healthy, well-balanced meals. She makes homemade lasagna and chicken primavera.

It's nice . . . having someone who cares enough to cook for you and make sure you're fed."

"Don't tell me how to live my life." The prick. I guess he hasn't kicked it old school and dined on candy and hard liquor in a while. His fucking loss.

"Just trying to look out for you is all."

Crossing my arms over my chest, I lean back. "You guys get Macey settled in today?"

"Yeah. It's a nice place she found, in a safe area. I think she's a little worried about how she's going to afford it without a job, but I cosigned the lease and told her I'll help if she needs it."

I nod. Knowing Macey, she'll find a way to make it all work, without anyone's help. It's just the kind of girl she is. God love her.

"How was her mood today?" I'm trying not to be terribly obvious, but the memory of our session is still buzzing through my veins, and I feel guilty I didn't pay any mind to aftercare. It went against everything I knew as a Dominant, but I was painfully aware I couldn't handle the level of emotional intimacy that comes along with it.

"What do you mean?" Hale asks, now helping himself to a handful of my candy that's scattered across the coffee table in a colorful mess.

I shrug, trying to downplay my concern. "Just curious after our session yesterday—"

I don't get to finish, because he rises to his feet, clenching his fists at his sides. "You fucking went through with that?"

"Of course I did. I told you I was going to."

"You're a selfish asshole, Reece. What the fuck?"

Confused, I stand as well. "I thought we both agreed it was better that I introduce her to the scene than some sadistic Dom doing God knows what with her." *Was he smoking crack when we met for lunch that day?*

"Don't you have enough subs on speed dial? Macey's my sister. Since I apparently didn't make it clear before, I don't want you messing around with my goddamn sister." His voice rises three levels, and if I had any neighbors, I'm pretty sure they'd be able to hear every word.

He said no sexual contact, and apparently he thought that was going to make me scrap the whole idea. Not that I abided by his request anyhow. The visual of Macey's full lips wrapped around the head of my cock is permanently burned into my brain. And I can't even find it in me to feel guilty about it. In fact, I want to do that again and again. *Shit*.

Realizing Hale's still fuming, still watching me and waiting for an answer, I grab my glass, knowing I'll need a refill to continue this conversation. "Another measure?" I ask, glancing down at his empty glass on the table.

"Answer the damn question," he barks.

I walk to the bar and pour myself another. "I'm not seeing anyone right now. Just Macey."

"You make it sound like an ongoing arrangement."

Turning back to face him, I try not to flinch

when I see the vein in his forehead that only appears when he's mad. Like fighting mad. *Shit*. This isn't what I anticipated when I told him to swing by tonight.

"It is. I promised her three sessions; I just don't know how she's feeling about continuing them. That's why I asked you what her mood was like. She kind of rushed out of here."

"If you did something . . . if you hurt her, so help me God—"

"I didn't. I'd never hurt her." The sincerity in my tone makes him pause, and he looks at me as if he's looking at me for the first time. For a second, I think he's going to see straight through me, that he's going to discover that I've held feelings for her all this time. But then he lets out a deep exhale and gestures for me to continue.

"So, what happened?" he asks, pressing his lips together.

I take a swig before continuing. "I didn't hurt

her. I just might have . . . pissed her off. Ended the session earlier than she probably expected."

"That's it? You cut it short?" This seems to make him happy, his tight posture relaxing just slightly.

Staring at my glass, I say, "I'm trying to be careful with her."

I don't explain that my concern has nothing to do with the fact she's his sister, and everything to do with protecting my heart. The damn thing got crushed the last time she walked away. I can't go through that again because this time, it would be much harder. She's living here, in the same city. I'll see her at holidays and parties, and fuck, will probably have to watch her get married. All at once I feel like punching something.

"You know my stance on this," Hale says with a no-nonsense glare. "No good can come of it."

I give him the nod he's looking for; he's one thousand percent right. "Understood."

He frowns and stands. Then without another

word, he makes his way to the door, our conversation and our evening over, it seems. The door closes softly behind him, and I'm alone once again.

Hale and I have never fought. Not once. I'm confused and feeling even more vulnerable than I imagined. When another Dom tells you you're in the wrong, you stop and take note. Period.

Alone in the quiet solitude of my apartment, I reflect on all the ways I've fucked up lately. First Chrissy asking why I've never settled down with a submissive, then my murderous feelings toward Oliver when he touched Macey, and now Hale questioning what I'm doing, coupled with my sullen mood after she moved out today.

I look down at my coffee table littered with colorful candies and an empty glass of Scotch. This is like a damn post-breakup pity party. All that's missing is the ice cream and cheesy romantic comedies. I need to fucking man up. I'm Reece-motherfucking-Jackson. I own Crave—Chicago's hottest sex club. I deliver the pleasure; I decide the punishments. I can't let one feisty girl who I used to be hung up on call the shots on our arrangement.

Through my confused fog, clarity emerges. I might have fucked up running from Macey like that yesterday. But in our next session, I will make damn sure I don't make the same mistake twice. She wants to experience this? Fine. I'll let her see every ounce of my depraved side and let her decide for herself if she can handle it.

Chapter Nine

Macey

I'm standing in the bathroom, arranging my toiletries on the little shelf above the sink, when my phone rings for the third time.

"Uh. Fine, I'm coming," I say to no one in particular, stomping across my new apartment to hunt for my cell phone. I find it underneath a pizza box that has sustained me for the last two days. I'm tired and irritable, considering all I've done over the past forty-eight hours is unpack boxes, scrub floors, wash windows, and stew over the memory of my awkward session with Reece.

When I strutted into his club on New Year's Eve looking for a good time, I never envisioned what could have happened. The Reece I remembered was a diligent, kind, and thoughtful lover. Not the kind of man to just walk away when it was over, leaving me to unbuckle the ankle restraints he placed me in, feeling confused and alone.

My phone displays a number I don't recognize.

"This better be important," I say.

"It is."

Reece's deep growl of a voice slams through me, and I have to brace myself with one hand against the counter. "Reece? Where are you calling from?"

"My office phone. You didn't answer when I called from my cell phone."

"I'm just in the middle of something. What's going on?"

"I'm calling about our next lesson."

He sounds so formal, as if we're scheduling a dentist appointment together or something. I want to give him a piece of my mind, and I will. But now isn't the time. I want to be face-to-face with him when I demand an explanation for the way he acted. He owes me that much.

"Okay. What about it?" My cool, detached tone matches his. Two can play at this game.

"Tomorrow. Eight o'clock. We'll meet in the lounge for a drink first."

"Fine. See you then."

I hang up, determined to show him once and for all that I might be submitting, but I'm no pushover. Deciding that I'm done with the unpacking and organizing, I text Brielle.

Hey . . . How about that margarita?

Thirty minutes later, we're sitting at a little place called the Lettuce Leaf, munching on organic chips and salsa, and sipping peach margaritas.

"I'm glad you texted," she says, taking another long sip of her icy drink. "Aren't these heaven?"

"They're delicious. I think I'm almost ready for another." I'm drinking embarrassingly fast, but dude, these are amazing. Like orgasms in a cup.

She watches me like she's looking for clues. "Is

something bothering you? You know, other than being cooped up in your new place?"

I shake my head. I don't know how much to tell her about Reece and me, though she did seem pretty intuitive the last time. Maybe it's the generous pour of tequila in my drink, but I'm looking across the table at Brielle, with her bright, inquisitive eyes and easygoing dressed-down style that includes a messy ponytail, and decide why the hell not open up to her?

"Reece and I had a session a couple of days ago."

Her brows rise up on her forehead. "A session?"

"Don't act so innocent. I know my brother's a member at Crave, so surely that must mean you've been well acquainted with the kink that goes on there."

She blushes and looks off in the distance. "I always wondered what Reece was into . . ."

"He was intense, unyielding, and when it was

over, boy was it over. He just left me in his private playroom and told me to get cleaned up."

Brielle frowns. "What about aftercare?"

"After what?"

She shakes her head. "Maybe that's just a Hale thing. Never mind. Continue."

"I just wanted to have a little fun, you know, blow off some steam, but now I'm questioning if I want to do that again. Sure, it was exciting. My heart was pounding a million miles an hour not knowing what was going to happen in that room, under his skillful hands, I just didn't expect to feel so . . . unsatisfied at the end."

Brielle chews on the end of her straw, looking thoughtful. "That's strange that he was so abrupt about it. You know, Hale says that Reece has never settled down, has never taken on a submissive, almost like he'd had his heart broken and swore off anything serious. Which doesn't make sense to Hale, because he says Reece never had anything serious enough to end badly. Although he did take his parents' divorce pretty rough."

Well, isn't she just a font of information. It's interesting about Reece's supposed lockdown of his heart. I get the sense he's closed off too. But why? It couldn't have been my relationship with him. He's the one who ended things. He could have had me any way he wanted me—geez, I delivered myself on a silver platter, but no dice. Besides, that was a lifetime ago. I'm sure he moved on. Many times.

"I'm not sure," I say, taking another long sip of my drink while I gesture to the bartender for another. Fuck it; I'll be taking a cab home anyway.

Brielle clears her throat, her expression thoughtful. "Reece turned to BDSM several years ago, and then opened his club a few years later. I don't know much of his past beyond what Hale's mentioned. Sorry I don't have any juicy gossip. I suck at girl talk."

I smile at her. "Well, I know something juicy."

"What's that?"

The bartender sets down two fresh peach margaritas, and I trade my empty glass for a full one. "He's hung like a damn horse."

Brielle chokes on her drink and coughs. "Seriously?"

I nod, a grin twitching on my mouth. "Seriously. That is one gargantuan slab of male virility. It's like a huge fucking cock."

"Oh my God." Brielle is chuckling behind her hand. "He's what . . . . six foot six?"

"Six four," I correct. But yeah, he's a giant. Built, muscular, handsome. And sweet, yet with a dark and troubled side I want to figure out. "And trust me, his cock is proportionate. It's intimating. I mean, what do I do with that?" Remembering back to the way I made him come so quickly with my mouth, a twinge of pride ripples through me.

"Good luck with that," she says, still flushed and grinning at me.

· · ·

With my shoulders back and my breasts thrust forward, I walk like I'm strutting down the runway at a major fashion show. Confidence exudes from every part of me, and I feel powerful and alive. Now that I know what to expect, I enter the club with more self-assuredness than before. My heels click across the floor as I head straight for the bar.

Spotting Reece at the bar with a Scotch in his hand, I can't help but remember the lesson he gave me on how to enjoy his favorite drink. He looks handsome but troubled with his broad shoulders pulled forward as he leans over the bar.

I stop beside him and lift myself onto the bar stool.

"What are you craving, sweetheart?" the bartender asks, stopping in front of me.

"One of those, please," I say, glancing at Reece's glass of Scotch.

Reece nods in approval as the bartender strolls away and grabs a bottle of Macallan, an expensive aged Scotch.

"Clever line. Is that your doing?" I ask, nodding after the bartender.

"The line? No, I paid a publicity company twenty thousand dollars to come up with that."

When it's placed before me, I take a small sip of the drink, letting the burn fade on my tongue before I swallow just like Reece showed me. We sip our drinks quietly, a strange energy burning between us. It's sexually charged, but there's something else too—something I don't quite understand yet, but want to.

"What did you do today?" he asks.

"Nothing much. Ran errands, then I got a manicure." I wasn't thrilled about the expense since I'm not working yet, but unpacking chipped my nails all to hell.

He lifts my hand to inspect my nails. "Still black," he says grimly, as if the dark color is a reflection on my mood.

"Yes," I answer, though he can plainly see the color hasn't changed.

The woman I saw in Reece's office struts past, her lingerie-clad hips swinging. She treats him to a coy smile, and he nods at her. A flash of jealousy flares inside me. I know she must be an employee of the club, but still, it makes me wonder if he has a past with her.

"I'm not here for your little games," I say, snatching his attention away from her like a little kid grabbing for her favorite toy.

"I thought that's exactly why you were here," he says, enjoying another sip of his drink.

Leveling him with an icy stare, I throw the rest of my drink back. "I'm here because I want a good time. And I think you want that too, need it."

He looks down at the bar. "What are you saying, Macey?"

"No holds barred. If we're doing this—let's do it. No cutting out early. No going easy on me. I want the full Reece Jackson experience." A smile lifts my mouth.

"You sure that's what you want?"

"Positive," I say, ignoring the wave of nerves fluttering in my belly.

"Then let's go."

Standing, he offers me his hand, and I take it, rising gracefully from the bar stool. Instead of heading for the elevator like before, he leads me to a stairwell that's deserted and quiet. Nothing but the sound of our footsteps cuts through the heavy silence.

When we reach his private room, we stop in front of the door and I turn to him. "Do you ever do this in your apartment?"

"No." Reece looks down at me. His expression is impassive, but his tone is harsh. "Do you remember the code?"

I nod, unsure how to feel about the knowledge that he doesn't bring women to his place. That's just weird.

"Your birthday." When I punch in the code on the keypad, the door clicks open to reveal the same quiet, dark, and sensual room I remember, and my heart rate kicks up immediately.

"Undress and wait for me on the bed," Reece says, his tone sure and steady.

This is Reece the Dominant, and I fucking love it. My belly is tingling with nerves, and I feel alive and eager.

"Yes, sir," I say, then bow my head and cross the room toward the bed.

After stripping off my jeans, socks, and shirt, I fold everything into a pile and place it on the dresser, leaving my bra and panties in place, remembering that he seemed to enjoy removing those himself last time. The soft sound of classical music comes from overheard, and I turn to see Reece adjusting the settings on a built-in stereo panel on the wall.

I sit on the end of the bed and wait for him. Watching him cross the room toward me is special form of torture. He's so handsome and strong, but with an underlying vulnerability that tugs at my heart. I can't help but recall my conversation with Brielle. There's a sadness to him I want to chase away.

When he pulls his long-sleeved Henley off over his head, I'm treated to the elaborate ink that decorates his right arm from shoulder to wrist. I haven't gotten the chance to fully explore it, but I want to. It looks delicious, and I'm eager to trace every inch of it with my tongue.

"You want to see them?" he asks, smirking at me.

"Can I?"

He shrugs. "Sure."

Taking his hand, I lift his arm. He lets me drink my fill, turning it to see the designs that wrap around his taut forearm and his thick bicep. There's a quote in what I think is Latin.

"What does it say?"

"It loosely translates to: Chase away the demons."

Oh.

Dark swirls of gray and black designs decorate his skin, perfectly drawn. Whoever the artist was, he or she was very talented. Nestled within thorns and leaves is a vivid red rose, the only pop of color on the whole piece. It's on his forearm, near the crook of his elbow, as if it's been deliberately placed in that sensitive spot. I can't help but feel this rose has a certain significance to him.

"A rose?" I voice my question, hoping my curiosity will be answered.

"Macey Rose."

Rose is my middle name, but there's no way he did this for me . . . is there? My heart is pounding, but before I can say anything more, the moment passes.

Reece leans over and grabs his toy bag. "You said no holding back this time, but I need to hear you say it. Are you sure that's what you want?"

Swallowing my nerves, I nod.

"Tell me," he says.

"I want this."

He's looking down at me so thoughtfully, and maybe it's this heavy moment, or maybe it's the beautiful rose permanently inked on his body that might be for me, but I want to kiss him.

Memories of our first kiss flash through me. It was raining out, pouring actually, and I was hiding behind my parent's shed as I tried to work up the courage to run toward the house. Reece came to check on me and help me inside. The way the rain had soaked his clothes, making them mold to every hard, muscled plane of his body, was too much. The secret attraction for each other we'd been fighting all summer seemed to boil over all at once.

I can't remember who made the first move, all I know is that suddenly our mouths were fused together while warm raindrops fell heavily on us. My fingers knotted in his soaked T-shirt while his tongue quested for mine. I remember my pounding heartbeat, and the damp flood of moisture between my legs when his teeth nibbled my bottom lip. His kiss was raw. Primal. And still the best kiss I've ever had.

We may be different people now, but that doesn't stop me from leaning in toward him and placing my palm against his cheek. "Can I kiss you?"

He lets out a long, slow exhale, but doesn't answer. "Lie down on the bed."

Confusion rushes through me, but I do as I'm told. Reece's fingertips skim over my belly, my hips, the pressure so light it tickles. His calloused fingertips are warm against my skin. It strikes me just how perfectly built for each other we are, his strength for my softness. I suck in a breath when he reaches the juncture between my thighs.

"Spread your legs for me. Show me that sweet little cunt," he says.

His words are so crass, and I've never been

spoken to like this before, but my body responds immediately. I'm warm all over, and between my legs grows damp.

"Beautiful," he growls, running the pad of his thumb between my folds, feeling the slick heat that's just for him.

I part my legs further. All my self-consciousness falls away at the appreciative tone in his voice and the hunger I see reflected in his eyes.

"I'm going to show you how to be a good submissive tonight. How to please me. Would you like that?"

"Yes," I answer honestly. The idea of pleasing him makes me feel hot all over. Maybe it's the way his tall, muscular frame looms over me, or that sexy-as-sin sleeve of dark tattoos, but I'm turned on and soaked already.

Shameless. But who cares.

When he removes a length of black rope from his bag, I present my hands to him, placing my wrists together in front of me.

"Good girl," he says, looping the rope over each wrist and securing them together. Once my wrists are secured, he places them over my head, up near the headboard. "Keep them up here."

Before I can even wonder what happens next, he lowers himself to the bed between my legs. "Just one little taste," he says, and before I can prepare myself, his mouth is on me, his tongue licking against my sensitive clit.

My hips shoot off the mattress and I cry out. I want to bring my hands to his hair, feel the soft strands between my fingers, but I keep my arms above my head, wanting to obey him and take the pleasure he's offering. Something tells me that maybe this is his way of making up for being an asshole last time.

"Fuck, you taste good," he murmurs with his mouth still against me. "I could eat this sweet pussy for hours."

Yes, please. My hips are circling of their own

accord, my breathy moans getting louder and louder, my orgasm getting closer, when he suddenly stops. He fucking stops.

A frustrated groan travels up my throat. I blink open my blurry eyes, trying to focus on him and figure out why for the love of God he'd stop.

"Not yet, princess. I'm just getting started, and you won't come tonight until I say so."

I take a deep breath, trying to calm my raging hormones. "I understand, sir. Tell me how to please you."

Rising to his knees, he flicks open the button on his jeans and takes out his thick, heavy cock, stroking it in his right hand.

God, that's sexy. I could watch him do this all night, but after a couple of slow strokes, he stops.

"You want to know how to please me? Turn over on your belly and show me that sexy ass of yours."

With my heart rate ratcheting up, I roll onto my

stomach and place my bound hands underneath me, lying with my knees bent so that my butt is up in the air. I should feel exposed and uncomfortable, but the appreciative murmur in his throat tells me that he fucking loves this view. He's always been an ass man. I guess some things never change.

"Have you ever done this before?" he asks.

"No, sir." I've never been interested. But with Reece, I find that I am.

I feel him, the heat of his broad body against me. His chest hovers over my back, and his thighs press against the back of mine as he leans over me. I tremble when his lips touch between my shoulder blades as he places a tender kiss there. I wanted to kiss him tonight, even asked him if I could, but it seems this is the only kind of kiss I'll get. Knowing that, I savor the press of his full mouth against my skin.

"I'm going to fuck this tight, virgin ass. And you're not going to come until I say so. Do you understand?"

"Yes," I croak. Nervous does not even begin to describe my state of mind. I'm about to tell him there's no way in hell I'm going to be able to come from this when I hear a low hum of vibration.

Wondering what's about to happen, I feel Reece's fingertips rub my back opening, warm and slippery with lubricant.

Oh. Hello there.

"Breathe for me," he whispers, placing another one of those sweet kisses against the back of my neck that make me feel too many things.

I try to focus—not on the man, but on the act, the mechanics of it all. I need to keep myself detached. When the broad head of his cock presses against my ass, I pull a deep breath into my lungs. There is no way in hell that's going to fit. That thing is gargantuan.

"Do you trust me?" he asks from behind me.

"Yes." There's no question, no hesitation on my part, and I sense that that pleases him.

"Then breathe and try to relax for me. I'm not going to hurt you. I know what I'm doing."

I don't want to think about all of the submissives who came before me, but perhaps he's right. His experience with women will be a benefit to me, if I let it.

"It's just I don't see how this will work. I've never . . . and you're . . ."

"Shh." He quiets me with another tender kiss pressed between my shoulder blades. "It's nothing that patience and a lot of lube can't solve. Plus you have full medical coverage, right?" He chuckles darkly, and I stiffen. "I'm kidding, babe. Relax. I know what I'm doing. I'm going to make this good for you."

I take a deep breath and try to relax. His finger is still stroking my asshole, and just as I'm getting used to the sensation, he moves the small buzzing toy—a vibrator—between my legs.

Unable to control myself, I moan.

"That feel good?"

"Yeah." *Fuck*. It really does.

He rubs the toy against my clit and pushes one finger inside my backside.

Oh. That's different, but it's more pleasurable than I imagined it would be. I move my hips back and forth, enjoying the dual sensations. Soon the wide head of his cock replaces his finger, and he pushes forward very slowly, letting me adjust to him.

"Fuck, Macey," he curses low under his breath.

I'm about to ask him what I've done wrong when he slides deeper. I lose my breath, along with my ability to speak. He fills me so completely; I'm totally at his mercy.

He grips my hip, pulling me back and forth on him as if I'm merely a vessel for his pleasure. "What is it about you? You make me lose myself." He grunts with each thrust, still keeping his magic little toy against me.

I don't answer. I can't, because suddenly I

realize how close I am to climaxing.

"Reece." I breathe his name out on a moan. "I'm going to come."

"Not yet," he says, his commanding tone returning.

I cry out, groaning his name and begging. "I need …"

"No fucking way. When you come, it's going to be on my tongue."

My hips buck wildly, and I'm struggling to hold back the most powerful orgasm of my life. It's almost painful. I bite my lip, crying out, tears stinging my eyes and my chest heaving.

Just when I can't take one more ounce of pleasure, he removes the toy from between my legs. *Thank fuck.* Then he rocks into me in a few short, uneven thrusts, and his thick cock pulses inside me as he lets go. His voice is a rough whisper as he climaxes, and I've never heard a more beautiful or desperate sound.

Slowly, he pulls himself free from my body. I feel tired and used, but in the most wonderful way. I collapse into a heap, my legs buckling under me.

Reece lifts me and turns me over, laying me on my back on the bed. His cock is still hard and huge, standing tall. With his pulse thumping in his neck, and the veins straining in his arms, he looks sexy and dangerous.

"Let me untie you first."

He works at the ropes around my wrists, and soon I'm free. My hands are cool and tingly as I stretch my fingers. Reece bends down and brings his mouth to my breast, taking one nipple in his mouth and sucking it firmly. My whole body is hypersensitive; I'm not going to last long.

Reaching between my legs, he slides one long finger inside me, and my pussy squeezes him. "Such a good girl, letting me fuck your ass like that." His hot mouth moves to my other breast.

"Please, I need to come," I beg.

"Only because you asked so nicely," he says, positioning himself between my parted thighs again. His wicked mouth devours me, licking in a rhythm that quickly brings me to the brink. With my hands now free, I push my fingers into his hair, tugging him closer. I moan his name as he sucks my clit into his mouth, devastating the last of my self-control.

Like the crash of waves against the shoreline, a powerful orgasm washes over me, pulling me under. I ride it, my body bucking from its power, my breaths coming hard and fast until I nearly hyperventilate. When the last spasms fade, I lay flat on my back, completely exhausted, my chest heaving with each breath.

It takes several moments for the haze of my orgasm to wear off, and when I come to, Reece has already risen from the bed and is yanking off a condom I didn't know he wore.

Irrational tears sting my eyes. *Dammit*. All I told him I wanted was some hot, sweaty fun. So why does his hit-it-and-quit-it mentality toward me hurt so much? Because we have a history, a deep shared connection that ended too quickly. I blink rapidly, trying to breathe deeply and calm down before I embarrass myself with a display of emotion that has no place in one of his scenes.

The faucet is running. Apparently Reece is washing his hands in the adjoining bathroom. When he emerges, he's fully dressed. He looks cool and composed, as if nothing significant just happened between. As if our being intimate was nothing to him.

He turns to face me, his face devoid of any emotion. "You did very well. You'll probably be a little sore tomorrow. A warm bath with Epsom salts will help."

I nod dumbly. I just want to be alone and try to process everything that's just happened between us. "Can I stay?" I tug the blanket up to my chin, curling onto my side.

"Of course you can. Stay as long as you like."

I turn away, shielding myself from the sight of

him.

"Are you okay?" he asks. There's a whisper of softness to his voice.

With tears in my eyes, I glance up and meet his worried gaze. "I'm fine." My voice is sure and steady, even if my body is still shaking.

A few moments later, the door closes softly behind him, indicating to me that if I ever held a piece of this man's heart, I certainly don't now. Feelings of pain and confusion flash through me, and I hug the pillow tighter, noting his scent still lingers. Why in the world I thought this would be all fun and games, I have no clue. Reece's rejection stings way more than Tony's cheating ever did. I rub at an achy spot in my chest, trying to figure out what in the fuck that dull throb is coming from, and how I ended up so far over my head again.

Shit.

When I finally work up the strength to move, I get dressed and head out, hoping to get out of this club without Reece spotting me. I've never been good at hiding my emotions, and I'm sure my sullen mood is written all over my face.

"Macey?" A woman's voice stops me in my tracks.

Shit. So much for escaping unnoticed.

I spin around to see Chrissy—one of the workers here—dressed in the same black lingerie as last time.

"Hello," I say, my voice hoarse.

"Hi there. Everything okay?"

She must have noticed my attempt at making a hasty retreat. I consider shoving off and telling her I'm in a rush, but as much as I don't want to admit it, this woman might know Reece better than I do. She could be a valuable source of information to me. And since I'm completely at a loss about what I just experienced with him, I stop and take a deep breath, trying to calm my nerves.

Taking a deep breath, I try to smile. "I'm fine, really."

Her gaze fixes on mine and her nose crinkles. "Are you sure? I saw Reece come out of his room looking . . . upset."

"We just . . . never mind. It's not important." I hate how true those words feel. In all the years I've known him, Reece has never made me feel as insignificant as he did just now. I blink back a fresh wave of tears.

She frowns. "You can talk to me, you know. I've worked here alongside him for years. I've got to know him pretty well. Maybe I can help."

"When did Reece get that rose tattoo?" I ask.

She lifts an eyebrow, considering it. "He's always had it. Since I've known him, anyway. He built the rest of his sleeve around that piece. I've always figured it was important to him, but ever the secretive type, he's never dished on its significance."

"I see." It makes me more curious than ever.

"You guys have been spending a lot of time together. Has he finally taken a submissive?"

"No, it's not like that. I'm new to all of this, and I honestly, I was just looking to blow off a little steam. It was supposed to be three lessons, and we've had two." Two insanely erotic lessons that were hot and should have been fulfilling. But they lacked any real intimacy, and have left me feeling more lost than ever.

There's a faraway look in her eyes. It's obvious she's recalling some memory of her and Reece. A fond one, if the slight smile on her red-painted lips is any indicator. "Is it still true?"

"What?"

"That he only fucks in the mouth or in the ass."

I shudder. *Holy shit.* That's . . . insane, if it's even true.

I hate that she knows so many intimate details about Reece—the man who's grown cold and distant in the years I've been away. I shrug. "Maybe." Despite that being exactly what our first two sessions consisting of, something in me doesn't want Chrissy knowing all the juicy details. Yet there's something more about the way she says it, as if it's a fact that he has some weird hang-up about sex. "Why would he do that?"

She sighs. "I asked him once. In my mind, the only reasoning could be that he didn't want to have sex where he could get a woman pregnant."

Interesting theory.

"But he scoffed at that and said it had nothing to do with it. I guess it's just a personal kink of his. Who knows?"

"So you and he . . ." I swallow the painful lump in my throat.

"No, not really. Nothing serious, anyway. We played a little a few years ago, but that was before I became an employee of the club. He runs a tight ship here and keeps everything professional. If you want something with him—something real—trust me, I'd never stand in your way. Besides, he doesn't see me that way."

It stings to know he's treated me exactly the

same as he would any submissive he took to his chambers for a session. But I'm not just any submissive. I'm not a submissive at all. And we have a history. We should mean more to each other than that. Yet, he didn't deviate one inch with me. *For* me.

At first I assumed it was because of some childish oath he made to Cameron. But now I'm beginning to see it's because maybe it's like Brie said—he's been hurt and has an ironclad wall up around his heart.

I still want the same thing I did six years ago. God, have I learned nothing? Despite my tough-girl persona, I'm still every bit in love with my older brother's, very unobtainable, best friend. *Shit*.

Chapter Ten

Reece

Just fucking awesome. Now Hale isn't answering my calls, and I'm positive it has everything to do with my *relationship* with Macey. I just wanted to congratulate him on his engagement properly, and invite him and Brielle out for a glass of celebratory champagne. I knew he was planning to propose, and I knew Brielle would say yes, but I haven't actually spoken to him in days. Since I'm unable to get through to him directly, I call his secretary to leave a message.

"Are you calling about tonight's engagement party?" she asks, interrupting me.

"Yeah, I am," I say with smug satisfaction. A sinner like me is destined for hell, anyway. What's one more lie?

"I've been getting calls all day. It's been moved to the Estate Gala ballroom due to room-size constraints."

"And that's at North Oaks Country Club?" I take a wild stab in the dark. It's the nicest place in the whole city.

"Yes, sir," she confirms.

"Great, thank you." I hang up, fuming and in disbelief that my supposed best friend wouldn't invite me to his own fucking engagement party. The cocksucker.

Next I call the North Oaks Country Club and find out the event begins at seven tonight. I grab the dry cleaning bag that contains my one and only suit, and toss it on the bed. Glancing at my watch, I see I'll have just enough time to shower and pick up a suitable engagement gift, before fighting the Chicago traffic to make it there on time.

When I arrive, I'm pleasantly surprised to be greeted by a smiling Brielle.

"You made it." She hugs me. "Hale said he didn't know if you'd be here."

I nod and return her smile. The asshole didn't even bother tell her that he snubbed me. "I wouldn't miss this for the world."

Hale stalks up, confusion etched across his face when he spots me. "Reece. You're here."

"You sound surprised, brother." Now I'm just toying with him. The fuckwad.

"I didn't know if you'd be able to tear yourself away from your activities at the club," he returns, scowling.

We're skirting around the elephant in the room. We both know we're talking about Macey, yet we're not.

"Of course I could. This is for you both." I hand him an envelope containing a check for a thousand dollars. There's nothing better to make him feel like shit for excluding me than cold, hard cash. "Congratulations."

He peeks inside the envelope and his eyes widen. "Can I have a word?" Tipping his head at the bar, he and I start toward it, leaving Brielle to wonder what's going on.

"What the fuck is this? You're trying to buy me off because you know I'm pissed about you and Macey?" he asks, shoving the envelope in my face.

"That's a gift. Keep it. I'm happy for you that you've found someone worthy of your affections this time. It has nothing to do with my involvement with Macey." That's the absolute truth.

The bartender heads over and we each order a drink, trying to figure out this new wedge between us. I thought things would blow over, but it's growing worse.

Hale picks up his drink and the glass of champagne he ordered for his bride-to-be. "You know where I stand. Don't fuck this up." He heads back toward Brielle, leaving me to wonder what I'm really doing here.

I sip my Scotch slowly, surveying the room. Christ, everyone's here. Oliver and Chrissy, and even a few members from the club are standing near the piano, chatting amiably. Everyone but me was included in the celebration, it seems.

When I spot Macey, it's like all the air has been sucked from the room. My breathing hitches, and my hands ache to touch her. She's stunning, entirely fuckable. She's heading toward the bar, but she hasn't seen me yet. Her gaze is on the floor, the long stem of an empty champagne glass between her fingers. She walks slowly, taking her time, and her eyes remain downcast as if she's deep in thought.

I hate that some of the lively spark she's known for seems to have slipped away. The urge to kiss her mouth, her neck, her chest flares inside me, and I have to tamp it down. Her hair is twisted into a fashionable knot at the nape of her neck, her dress is a deep plum color and strapless, drifting all the way to the floor. Her nails are still painted black.

She looks incredible. I haven't seen her since I left her after our scene, and it strikes me again just how gorgeous she really is with that understated beauty. But leaving the way I did was the only option. Still, it torments me that I couldn't provide her with aftercare, that I couldn't be the one to draw her a warm bath and shampoo her hair. Nothing good would come of such intimacy, though, which was why I forced myself to leave.

"Hello," I say when she's closer, and her head snaps up.

"Oh. Reece." She stops where she's standing, as if she's afraid to come any closer to the dangerous and unpredictable animal.

"Hi." So much for a tempting pickup line. This woman turns me into a caveman capable only of uttering only single-syllable words. I've been trying to clear my head of the images of her hands bound with my ropes, the luscious spill of cleavage over her lacy bra, the expression on her face as I pushed her to her limits as she tried to hold back her orgasm. She did beautifully, and damn, she felt even better than perfection. But now, standing close enough that I can smell her sweet scent, I know I'm fighting a losing battle.

She lets out a deep exhale. "I didn't think you were coming."

"I wasn't invited."

Her brows squeeze together. "Seriously?"

"I'm always serious." I take another sip of my Scotch.

"So, I'm not the only one mad at you then," she says confidently, her stance straightening.

"You're mad?" This is news to me.

"You're a selfish asshole and an idiot. Chrissy told me about your kink. I feel like a fool. I thought our history meant . . . You know what? Never mind, I don't want to start a fight at my brother's party."

"My kink?" Now I'm really fucking confused.

She lowers her voice. "You only fuck in the mouth or the ass." Her tone is biting.

She's looking at me as if this information is disgusting, or like she feels sorry for me. But what am I supposed to say?

"It's been that way for a long time, yes." It's just one of the tactics I employ to ensure I don't fall for a woman. No sharing a bed, no intimacy, no sex. At least, not in the traditional sense. I hate the way her worried gaze latches onto mine, as if she's trying to solve a riddle. "You thought I was going to make love to you? Sorry, sweetheart, I'm not that guy anymore. This is me. Take it or leave it."

"I'll leave it. Good luck." And with that, she lifts her chin and strides away, her heels clicking across the floor as her long, graceful legs carry her toward the exit.

Fuck. Why do I feel like someone's punched me square in the chest? Rage boils unchecked inside me, and I want to hit something.

I down my drink, and am about to make a hasty exit myself when Oliver approaches.

"How are things progressing with Macey?" he asks, planting himself on the bar stool next to me.

"Just fucking terrific," I lie, poorly. I couldn't

wipe the grimace off my face right now if I tried.

"Sarcasm. Another defense mechanism?"

I narrow my eyes at him. "Careful. I've already taken shit from Hale tonight, and now Macey. Do you really want to fuck with me right now?"

Oliver orders a bottle of beer when the bartender approaches, but I know this conversation is far from over. His nostrils are flared, and a vein throbs at the base of his neck. "Listen. For once in your goddamn life, listen to me."

He's never taken on a rough tone with me, never been anything over than jovial. My head is spinning. "What the fuck have I done to piss you off?" Suddenly it strikes me, and I let out a bark of laughter. "Don't even tell me you're pissed off I kicked you out of that scene with Macey?"

"Of course not. God, will you listen to yourself?" He sets his beer down on the bar top and turns to face me, his eyes locked on mine and his expression serious. "I've known you for years, Reece. I've listened to the rumors, I've watched you take subs into your private room. In all that time you've never once asked for my help. But then suddenly you did, and I knew Macey was different. Just like that. I could see it in the way you looked at her, in the careful way you were with her. It wasn't a game to you. You touched her like her skin was something to be worshipped, like her body the most precious thing to you. And you looked like you wanted to murder me when I touched her. This girl means something to you. Don't try to deny it."

"She did. A long time ago. Not now. Not anymore. Besides, Hale would never fucking allow it, so it doesn't even matter." Something tells me if she didn't just walk away from me, it probably would have fucked up my friendship with him for good.

"I know you want everyone to see you as this successful business owner and in-control Dominant. And you are those things—no question. But what I see is a man running from his past."

I want to scream at him, to tell him that he's

wrong, to knock him on his ass. But fuck, this is *Oliver*. He's practically a therapist—a sex therapist, but whatever. The guy knows his shit. That's why he works for me. It's why his waiting list for new clients is more than six months long.

"Fight for her. Go after her, talk to her. I know she means something to you."

"Yeah, but is it worth fucking up my friendship with Hale?"

He gazes at me like he feels sorry for me. "If she's worth it, you'll figure it out."

I feel like someone stomped on my chest. It's hard to breath, and even harder to see straight. "I have to go." I don't know where; I just know I need out of this suit and tie that's trying to strangle me.

On my cab ride home, my mind is whirling. I consider texting Macey, just to check on her, to try to understand what I did wrong. All she wanted was a fun hookup, and I thought that's exactly what I gave her. But then I realize texting would be a pussy move. I need to call her. Hear her voice.

It's about to go to voice mail when she finally picks up.

"What do you want, Reece? I'm tired. It's been a long day."

"Just wanted to check on you. Are you home?"

"Yes. I'm in bed with a bag of microwave popcorn, about to start that new thriller everyone's been talking about."

"Are you still mad?" I ask, holding my breath. She doesn't seem mad. Then again, she did run out of her brother's engagement party after confronting me. I'm beginning to realize I don't understand the first thing about women.

"More like disappointed. Confused."

"I take it there won't be a third lesson."

"No." Her tone is final.

Something deep inside of me snaps, and I can't tell if it's disappointment or relief. "I'm sorry."

"No, it's my fault. I don't know why I thought

we could pick up where we left off. You're right. You're not that guy anymore."

A little piece of my heart breaks hearing her say those words. It's what I wanted, what I worked toward ever since she left, but now it seems I've locked my heart down so completely, I'm not even capable of giving her what she needs. Even when I need the exact same thing.

"Good night, Macey. Enjoy your movie."

"Good-bye, Reece."

Chapter Eleven

Reece

I hit the treadmill hard, pushing myself with my arms pumping, my lungs heaving with the need for oxygen. Loud, angry music blares in my ears. I've been fighting with myself for three days. I've hardly slept, I've hardly eaten, and I haven't had any desire to take a submissive back to my playroom. I'm miserable all the time, and fuck if I know what to do about it.

Pressing the INCLINE button, I pump my legs faster to sprint up the hill to escape the recrimination playing inside my mind. Oliver's words from the engagement party swim in my head. Macey's defeated tone replays over and over. Hale's anger. Shit, even Chrissy was shooting me evil glares that night once Macey stormed out.

I hate people pointing out my weaknesses; maybe that's the Dominant within me. Then again, maybe that's just part of being a man. We're supposed to be the stronger of the species. We should protect and cherish what's ours. But Macey isn't mine. In fact, she wants nothing to do with the man I've become, which is a harsh fucking wake-up call.

All this time, my goal has been to prove to myself that I can enjoy some carnal pleasures with the girl from my past who once gutted me. Yet, achieving that goal has provided me with zero pleasure. Well, that's not entirely true. Seeing Macey naked and bound in my playroom was pretty fucking awesome. But I fucked it up. All this time, my goal has been about protecting myself. Oliver was right.

Fuck.

A real Dominant isn't concerned with his own needs. He puts his partner's well-being and satisfaction above his own. I never did that with Macey. I was so worried about getting hurt again, I closed myself off. She was right—I treated her like any other sub, only worse.

Hitting the red STOP button, I step off the treadmill and fight to catch my breath. I grab my hand towel and use it to mop up the damp sweat on the back of my neck. Color flashes in my vision. She's everywhere it seems. Marked on my body for all of eternity.

Glancing down at the blood-red rose tattooed on my forearm, I know what I need to do.

I grab my phone and dial Hale. "Hey, man, I'm sorry, can we talk?" I say without taking a breath. At least he answered. It's a start. *I hope.*

"Not now." His tone is clipped.

He's going to make me grovel, and damn, I'm all too willing to do it. "I said I'm sorry, dude. I want to talk to you about—"

"It's Nana. She's in the hospital. She's been in ICU for two days . . ." His voice cracks, and he doesn't continue.

He doesn't have to. Nana is like a second mother to him and Macey. The only family they have left in this world.

"Which hospital? I'm on my way."

• • •

Running down the hospital corridor, I nearly plow into a parked wheelchair. *Geez, take a breath.* I slow myself down enough to read on the sign that the intensive care unit is on the sixth floor. Jabbing the button for the elevator repeatedly, I shift my weight from foot to foot, wondering if the stairs would be any faster.

Finally the elevator car arrives and delivers me to the sixth floor. There's a private waiting room for family with someone in the ICU, which is a good thing, because I realize I don't know Nana's first or last name when I check in at the reception desk. I head down the too-quiet hallway and enter the waiting room at the end of the hall. It's there I find Macey, alone and slumped in a plastic chair.

"Pancake?"

Her head lifts from its resting place on her arm, and her eyes are red and watery. She looks like hell, and something inside me clenches. "What are you doing here?" she asks, blinking up at me.

I cross the room in three long strides and draw her up into my arms. I pull her in firmly against my chest, and given our height difference, her feet dangle inches from the floor. For a second there, I think she might fight me, but instead she collapses against my chest, burrowing her face against my neck, and lets me hold her. It feels like coming home, as if this was the missing piece the entire last six years. But I don't let myself focus on that for long.

"How is she?" I ask.

Macey sniffles and lifts her head from the warm spot she's claimed as her own. "She's eighty years old. They're trying to prepare us for the worst."

"Christ." It's worse than I thought. "Any news on what happened?"

She nods. "They think it was a stroke. Right

now, she's in a sleep-induced coma while they try to figure out what kind of damage the stroke may have caused."

"I'm sorry, sweetheart." I tug her toward me again, and her warm body forms to mine. She makes a small murmuring sound of appreciation. "Have you seen her yet?"

"Yes, and there are so many machines and tubes, I almost fainted. It's horrible seeing her that way."

"I'm here now. I've got you." I ease us down onto the loveseat and continue holding her hand. "Why are you here alone? If I'd known . . ."

"Cameron and Brie went to the café to get more coffee. He sucks at just sitting here."

"I see."

Macey and I make small talk about inconsequential things like the weather and her new apartment. She tells me that she interviewed for a great job at a news station, then fills me in on the snafu when they first arrived at the hospital. The well-meaning hospital staff weren't going to let Hale and Macey see her. They have some immediate-family-only rule. But you don't come between an alpha male and his nana. Hale now has the nurses providing regular updates and extra-attentive care to Nana. *Thank God.*

I just listen and nod and let Macey talk, sensing it's therapeutic for her. Sitting in silence when you've received bad news only makes your head churn with possibilities, most of which are negative.

Hale and Brielle soon return with steaming paper cups of coffee in hand. They hand one to Macey, who shakes her head. She slumps against me, resting her head on my shoulder. Hale lifts an eyebrow in my direction, but doesn't say anything.

Being here with Macey, taking care of her this way, sparks a thousand memories. Watching her eyes fill with tears as she blinks them back and tries to be strong, reminds me of not so long ago when she and Hale got the devastating phone call that no one should ever have to get. I held her through the hurt and the tears, and when her tears dried up weeks later, I'd grown accustomed to having her in my arms, to being the one to quiet her fears, and tell her everything would be okay. It seemed natural that our relationship would evolve from there.

I realize they've been here in this little room, worried sick, for two days. I take in her rumpled clothes and dark-circled eyes. "Have you eaten? Slept?"

She frowns, but doesn't answer.

"I think you need to get some sleep, in a real bed, and a meal in you. It will make you feel better. Come on." I rise to my feet, offering her my hand. "Let me take you home."

"No, I can't leave Nana."

"Just for a couple hours, then I'll bring you back."

Hale glances at me, and we communicate without speaking. Our disagreement momentarily aside, this is about what's best for Macey. Hale nods in her direction, encouraging her. "Let Reece take you home, Mace. Just to shower and rest."

She sighs, but gives him a tight nod and takes my hand. "Okay."

This is what she needed me to do all along. Take control and look after her needs. That damn throbbing pain is back in my chest.

The drive to her apartment is quiet as Macey stares out the window, obviously worried. After she showers, I tuck her into her unmade bed and tug the fluffy white duvet up to cover her.

She lets out a gentle sigh. "You'll wake me in a few hours, and take me back to the hospital?"

Her eyes lock onto mine, and I know she's putting her trust and faith into me when I've let her down the last few times we were together.

"Yes, of course I will."

She closes her eyes and rolls onto her side, hugging the pillow to her chest.

I gaze down at her a moment, hating how I've

let her down. She said she wasn't mad, just disappointed in me, but I never wanted to be a source of disappointment for her. She has no job, a cheating ex, and a sick nana to stress over. I don't want to add any more stress to her life. I just want to be here. For her. With her.

I head out into the living room and sink down onto the couch. I lay my head on the armrest of the sofa, and as the minutes tick past, I realize that I want to be in her life. For real. Without any of the Dominant, macho bullshit to protect my heart. I just want her. I always have.

She's the one girl I never forgot. And trust me, I tried. For years I tried to wipe my brain clean of the memories of her sweet and loving nature, her kindness, her spark. I sought out new companions to replace those memories with dirty ones. Apparently it didn't work, because I still want her every bit as much as I did before. Maybe even more.

But she thinks I'm a complete prick, so what am I supposed to do?

• • •

While Macey slept, I attempted to make the banana pancakes she once made for me, but it ended with a mixing bowl of batter and a few burnt pancakes dumped down the trash before she woke. I don't know how to cook, and apparently it's harder than they make it look on TV. By the time I hear her stirring, I have takeout waiting for us on the counter, and I'm hoping it's the thought that counts.

Tentative footsteps cross the wooden floor as Macey enters the kitchen. "That smells good." Her eyes wander over the white pizza box on the counter. It seems she wants to look anywhere but directly at me.

Fuck, I wonder if this will get easier over time.

I shift a step toward her. "I hope you still like ham and pineapple."

She nods. She's got sleep lines across one cheek, and her long hair is tied up in a messy bun, but she looks gorgeous. Natural.

"And there's salad too." I grab the plastic bag on the counter and remove two side salads and a variety of dressing containers. I wasn't sure which she liked.

"I hate salad." She smiles wryly.

The mood lightens immediately, and my posture relaxes. "I do too." I set the containers of salad aside and grab two plates while she opens the pizza box and places a slice on each of our plates.

We eat sitting together in the living room while her TV plays some daytime game show that neither of us is familiar with. We make small talk about the contestants, but otherwise eat mostly in silence. Things between us are still strained, but this isn't the time to discuss that. Her thoughts are on Nana, as they should be.

After our meal, I drive her back to the hospital. Hale and Brielle are just leaving her room, and there are tears glistening in Brielle's eyes.

I take Macey's hand and hold it tenderly, as if that will shield her from whatever bad news we're about to hear. "What's going on?" I ask when we get closer.

They share a happy look. "She's awake. And talking. They think the damage from the stroke is minimal."

Macey practically sags with relief against me. "Thank God. Can I see her?"

Hale nods. "Yes. For a few minutes. She still needs her rest."

Assuming it's family only, I'm about to let Macey's hand go when she tugs me along with her toward Nana's room. It signals to me that I still mean something to her, that maybe she still needs me in her life. Or maybe she's just afraid to go in alone.

I haven't seen Nana in a long time, since last Christmas, I think, when she gave me the most hideous orange-colored hand-knit sweater. But as soon as my eyes land on her, my knees weaken. Her normally mocha-colored skin is ashen and pale, and a variety of tubes and wires connect her to a multitude of machines. The soft hum of the devices and the beeping in the background do not create a soothing environment. My grip tightens on Macey's hand.

"Nana . . . ," she says softly, and her voice breaks.

"Come here, child," Nana whispers weakly.

Macey's death grip on my hand means that I'm tugged along with her to the side of Nana's hospital bed.

Macey and Nana hold hands, and we stand there in silence as the two woman just study each other, both with tears in their eyes. It's a heavy moment, and I have no fucking idea what I'm supposed to say. Nothing seems right, so I stay quiet.

"You scared me," Macey says, her voice shaky as a tear slips from her eye.

Nana frowns. "I'm not going anywhere. These doctors are just worrywarts."

Macey smiles and leans down to kiss Nana's forehead. "You better not go anywhere."

Nana's eyes land on me next, and I stiffen. I feel as though she can see straight through me, like she can read all of my intentions. A pang of fear flashes through me, and I want to hide the depraved man I've become from her all-knowing eyes.

Then a slow smile lifts her mouth. "I always knew you two would end up together."

Macey opens her mouth to correct her, but I give her hand a firm squeeze.

"I'll always be here for Macey," I say forcefully, filling my words with resolve.

Macey glances up at me curiously. Tears are still glistening in her eyes, and I don't know if the emotion is for me or for her nana.

The last time we were together we fought at Hale's engagement party, and she looked sickened by my strange kink. I used her body in thoughtless ways, and left her afterwards naked and alone. I'm not proud of myself, and even though I know I can't fix the past with one declaration, I hope it's a start.

I lace my fingers with hers, unwilling to let her go.

Chapter Twelve

Macey

It was sweet what Reece did for me—coming to the hospital, sitting with me, listening to my nonsense, comforting me with his presence insisting that I go home and rest, and then accompanying me into Nana's room. He was there for me when I needed it, but I can't mistake that one act of kindness for something it's not. I gave him a chance, and he showed me who he really is now. I hate that he's this damaged man now, incapable of a real, loving relationship with a woman. Both Chrissy and Brielle tried to warn me. But the stubborn side of me, all gusto and bravado, wanted to fun some kinky fun. Too bad that didn't work out.

Still, I have a lot to look forward to. There are a lot of good things happening, like the job at the news station I started yesterday with a boss who seems like she'll be a great mentor, and Nana is recovering better than the doctor's expected. Still, I can't seem to shake the black cloud following me around.

I grab my purse and keys, and head for the door. I'm meeting Brielle for a celebratory drink tonight. She said she wanted to congratulate me on my new job. If it meant free margaritas, I don't need a formal invitation. Besides, maybe some alcohol will numb the pain I feel whenever I think about Reece.

When I arrive at the little Mexican restaurant, Brielle is already seated at a high-top table in the bar area, so I make my way over to her. The server approaches just as I do.

"Two peach margaritas, ladies?" he asks.

"It's like they really get me here." I smile and nod at him.

Brielle giggles and tells him, "Yes, plus an order of chips and salsa, please."

He scurries away, and I take my seat across

from her. It feels good being here in her presence, and I'm happy that we're starting to build what I know will be a real friendship.

"How was day two at the new job?" she asks.

"It was great. I think I'm really going to like it there. Good boss. Good assignments so far."

She frowns. "Then why do you look so defeated?"

"No, we're not talking about that tonight. We're going to have fun. We're going to discuss you and my brother, and wedding plans and babies."

She smiles at me and pats my hand. "We're not getting married until next summer. We want it to be a small affair, so we have plenty of time for wedding planning, and babies are still a ways off. Listen, I know something happened between you and Reece, and I'm here if you want to talk."

"Thanks. I appreciate that. I'm not sure if I'm ready to go there yet. I still have some healing to do."

The server delivers two margaritas and a basket of chips with salsa, and I waste no time pulling my glass toward me. Swirling my straw in the icy concoction, I can't stop my thoughts from wandering to Reece—his strong, muscular frame, that sleeve of sexy tattoos, and the pain I saw buried in his gaze whenever he met my eyes.

It's like he was trying to hold himself back from me, like he purposefully distanced himself from feeling anything for me. Why would he do it? It's not like he's in love with me all these years later.

Unless . . . he still feels something for me, just as I do for him.

No. That's crazy. It's just wishful thinking on my part, the romantic side to me that wanted to believe the cheating ass Tony was boyfriend material. Just because I want it to be real doesn't mean it is.

Shaking myself free of my thoughts, I say, "I

just don't understand it. I thought things between us were going to be light, casual, and fun, only that's not how it turned out at all."

"I know, sweetie. Reece is a complicated man. He and Hale have been fighting, and I hate it."

Something about that strikes me as odd. "They shouldn't still be fighting. I thought Hale would be happy that Reece and I done. I'm sure Hale will get over it, if he isn't already."

She chews on the end of her straw. "I don't think so. Reece called last night, and he's coming over to talk to Hale tonight."

"About what?"

"You."

This makes no sense. Reece and I done. "What's there to talk about?"

She shrugs. "Why don't you come over and find out?"

"I couldn't do that. Could I?"

Brielle smiles wryly. "Listen, you know both of these men claim they like submissive women, but I know what they really like is a woman with some spunk. Some fire, some gusto. It makes them feel like a big, bad alpha when they take charge in the bedroom. There's no reason why you shouldn't come over tonight and face him. You don't have to cower away, or fade into the background."

"I'm going to need a couple more of these then." I sip my margarita while Brielle gestures for another round to our server.

Chapter Thirteen

Reece

I woke up the last three mornings with my hand under the sheets, stroking my cock while I dreamed of being buried inside Macey. Maybe I just needed to do it—get her alone, and get her out of my system once and for all. That would fix this shit. Then again, maybe I'm just lying to myself.

"Reece?" Oliver pokes his head inside my office, pulling me from my thoughts.

"Yeah?" I glance up from my desk and my neck cracks. I haven't spoken to him in days, not since that showdown at the engagement party where he called me out.

"There are two new submissives here— smokin' hot too—who are asking to see Reece Jackson. You want me to call upstairs and have your private room prepared for a ménage scene?"

Normally the idea of two beautiful woman willing to submit to me would make my dick hard, but right now? I might as well be dead for all the interest I have. "No. I'm busy."

Oliver's eyes widen. "Too busy for pussy? That's a first." He chuckles.

"When I finish up my work here, I'm headed to Hale's. I need to clear the air between us once and for all. We need to talk this shit out, or do whatever it is guys do when they've been fighting."

"And what about Macey?" Oliver puts on a fake smile and crosses his arms over his chest.

Tired of him harassing me about this, I massage my temples. "What about her?"

"You're not seriously still going to try and pretend you're not in love with her, are you?"

That stabbing pain flickers inside my chest. "Get to the goddamn point," I bark.

"You need to tell Hale how you feel about her."

"Go take care of our guests, Oliver." I glance

back at my laptop and continue my work, ignoring him until I see him leave from the corner of my eye. *Nosy bastard.* If only he wasn't right.

• • •

"Where's Brielle tonight?" I ask Hale, admiring the view from their new thirtieth-floor condo in the heart of downtown. City lights twinkle below, and the dark waters of Lake Michigan glimmer in the distance. There are touches of both him and her throughout the tastefully decorated space.

"She's actually out with my sister. Girl time, or something."

"Hmph."

"Something on your mind, man?" Hale comes to stand beside me at the floor-to-ceiling windows in the living room, and hands me a drink.

I take a large gulp, the liquor burning my throat as I swallow it for courage before meeting his eyes. "I wanted to come here tonight to clear the air between us. I know you didn't want me messing around with Macey, but I came to you first, if you recall. And that was pretty fucked up not inviting me to your engagement party."

Hale lets out a heavy sigh. "I know, and I feel like shit about that, actually. Your gift was very generous. Thank you again."

"This isn't about the gift. I need to know that we're good."

"Come sit down." Hale heads to the leather sofa, and I sit down in a chair across from him. Once we're settled, he lets out a long sigh. "Macey's the only family I have. When my parents died, it changed me, made me grow up in a lot of ways I wasn't ready for. And even if I wasn't old enough to become Macey's legal guardian, in my mind, I was. She was my responsibly. Her education, her well-being, who she hung out with— all of it became my job to know. Back then she actually spent most of her time with either me or you, and I never worried about her. I knew you would look out for her as if she was your own sister."

I inwardly cringe. I never saw Macey as anything close to a sister. No, my intentions were much more sinful than that. Feeling worse than ever, I focus on Hale's words once again.

"But that was then, and you were different then. And it's not just because of your interest in BDSM these last few years; you were different as a person. You laughed more, you smiled, you took more chances. You had more fun. These days you're all brooding and hot-tempered, and not looking for anything more than a weekend plaything to take into your private room at the club and do God knows what with them, if the rumors are true. I want more for my sister. I hope you understand."

"Of course I understand. I know you want what's best for Macey. I get that." *But so do I.*

He smiles at me sadly. "You've changed. You've become this lost, broken man."

"First Oliver, and now you," I mutter, getting

really fucking tired of people looking at me like a lost puppy who needs saving.

"Oliver?" Hale's eyebrows lift.

"Nothing. He called me out for something similar."

Even though I'm trying to downplay it with Hale, Oliver's words are still ringing in my head. *You're in love with her.* That twisting feeling in my chest is back. I might need to get that checked out.

Or maybe I just need to face reality. Macey could forever be the one who got away, unless I could do something about it. Tonight.

Hale's watching me with a serious, solemn expression. "I guess what I'm saying is that I want the very best for my sister. Nothing against you, because you're my best friend, but I don't think you can offer her everything she deserves."

His accusations sting, and I can't resist biting back. "Have you asked Macey what she wants? What she thinks she deserves? Don't you want your sister to be happy? Have you asked her why she came to Crave?"

He tilts his head toward me and narrows his eyes. We square off this way, neither of us speaking or even blinking as the energy around us changes to something tense.

"I just don't want to see her get hurt," he says at last, his voice softer.

He's right. Hot guilt flashes through me. All these years of keeping something this monumentally big from my closest friend suddenly feels wrong. Beyond wrong. Deceitful. *Sinful*.

"Listen, there's something I need to tell you." My heart picks up speed, banging painfully against my ribs.

Hale leans forward, listening intently.

"Macey and I . . . years ago . . ." Embarrassed, I give him a pleading look. "Shit, don't hit me, okay?"

"Damn it. Just get it out, Reece."

I take a deep breath and release it slowly. "I loved her back then."

"Wow." He rakes his hands through his hair and leans back in his seat. "That's not what I expected to hear you say. I knew you guys were close back then, but—" His eyes widen, then narrow suspiciously on me. "Wait, you loved her like a sister, or something more?"

"More." *Much more.*

Speaking that one word removes a weight from my chest, a weight I've carried around for years. There's so much I want to tell him, to get off my conscience. I want to tell him that I was madly, deeply in love in Macey, that I wanted to be her first lover, but I resisted out of respect for my friendship with him. And because of that, I was fucking shattered when she left for college in the fall. That I've turned to BDSM to ease the pain of losing her.

"And now?" He's gazing at me thoughtfully, as if he's trying to piece everything together.

Before I can answer, the front door opens, and

a burst of feminine laughter spills into the room as Brielle and Macey enter the condo. Macey's gaze drifts over to me and her smile instantly fades.

That hurts worse than the punch I was anticipating from Hale earlier.

Brielle grins at us both and crosses the room, bending down to plant a kiss on Hale's lips.

"You taste like peaches," he murmurs.

"Behave." She gives him a flirty wink.

"Did you ladies have a nice time?" Hale asks.

Macey sits down in the chair beside mine, and just her physical nearness makes my heart beat faster. It's always been that way, though. She affects me on a chemical level, one that I've never been able to explain.

"Yes, it was fun," Macey says.

"Macey got a new job, and we were out celebrating," Brielle adds to fill me in.

"Congratulations."

"Thank you." Macey meets my eyes quickly, and then dips her chin toward the floor as if she's just lost some of her nerve.

I glance over at Brielle, who's watching us like we're the featured entertainment. All that's missing is the popcorn.

"Let me see that big rock." I reach out to Brielle, embarrassed that I was so damn distracted at the engagement party, it never even occurred to me.

Brielle places her left hand in mine and flashes the sparkly, round-cut diamond that looks classic and perfect on her finger.

I grin up at her. "The bastard has good taste."

"Thank you." She smiles and kisses my cheek. "Hale? Join me in the kitchen for a minute?"

"It would be rude to leave our guests," he says evenly as his gaze bounces between Macey and me. He's obviously trying to figure out where things stand between us, and what's been going on right under his nose. The bomb I just dropped on him is obviously still ringing loudly in his head.

"Since when am I a guest?" Macey asks, that spark of hers shining brightly.

"Hale, dear. *Now*," Brielle says.

He rises to his feet and follows her to the kitchen on the other side of the condo.

"Dom, my ass," I mutter under my breath.

Macey chuckles, lightening the mood for a second before she eyes me with suspicion. "What are you doing here, Reece?" It's as though she knows I just bared my soul to Hale, or at least attempted to.

"I came here intent on telling Hale what I want, and I wasn't leaving until he understood it."

Her nose crinkles as if she wants to understand, but doesn't. "And you guys are good?"

"I think so."

I glance into the kitchen to see Hale looking our way, still closely watching my interaction with

Macey. Part of me can't believe I came here to openly square off with him. I hadn't gotten the chance to say everything I wanted to, but I know I will. I'll set this right. These last few weeks have been eye opening. The people in my life who've forced me to take a good, hard look in the mirror showed that I don't like the man I've become.

"Listen, Macey, there are some things I need to apologize for."

"I'm listening," she says, folding her hands in her lap.

Fuck, where do I begin?

I regret that I didn't kiss her in our sessions. I regret the rough treatment I showed her body. Most of all, I regret letting her walk away six years ago. If she gives me another chance, and I pray she does, I want her stretched out in my bed, no ropes and no toys. Just pleasure and intimacy I've craved for six long years. I need to say good-bye to the man I once was, because if we do this, there will be no going back.

"I loved you back then. You knew that, right? I never said the words, but—"

"Yes, I knew." Her voice drops, and her eyes glisten with moisture.

"And it fucking gutted me when you left."

Her brows pull together. "You're the one who helped me fill out my college applications, practically pushed me out of the nest."

"I know. And I'd do it again in a heartbeat, because you were destined for more. I wasn't going to be the prick who held you back from achieving it."

"Yeah, some success story I turned out to be," she says quietly under her breath.

"Don't you dare define yourself by one failed relationship and a job that was going under. You fled when you needed to, and you're bouncing back just fine."

"I guess so."

"What I really want to apologize for is our sessions. You scared me. You strolled into my club, so cool and confident, and you knew exactly what you wanted. I made a bargain with myself that I wouldn't get attached, or feel anything for you again. I tried to treat you like any other sub, but it was quite obvious that you weren't."

"No, I'm not a submissive. It was a stupid idea, stupid of me to think we could do this without feelings getting involved. And stupid to think I could play the role of the kind of woman you like."

"You're the only kind of woman I like. All of this—the club, the toys—it was all meant as a distraction. I needed it like I needed air."

"What are you saying, Reece?"

If she trusts me enough to do this, I'm packing up all the impersonal BDSM implements I've used as a crutch. And not as some grand gesture, but because I want to. We won't need any blindfolds or handcuffs because I'll want her to see me, to touch me. It scares me, but it's what I want. And if she wants toys in the bedroom, we'll buy them together.

"Come outside on the balcony with me?" I want to get away from the curious ears of Hale and Brielle, who are standing only twenty feet away. Macey rises from the chair, and I grab the throw blanket from the back of the couch and wrap it around her shoulders. She hugs the blanket to her and follows me out onto the balcony. I slide the glass door closed as Macey stands near the railing, looking out at the spectacular view.

For a moment we just listen to the city noises below. The hum of traffic. A police siren fading in the distance. The whoosh of wind that lifts her hair from her neck.

It's January in Chicago, and barely thirty degrees out. Our breathing comes out in soft puffs as the warm air contrasts with the cold. I want to pull her into my arms and hold her small frame against mine, but I know I've lost that right.

"I wanted to properly apologize for the way I

treated you. I shouldn't have left you alone like that after our sessions. But I hope you understand now that I needed to get away. I couldn't seem to separate the emotion from the sex."

She turns to face me, her blue eyes sparkling in the moonlight. "Neither could I. That's why I didn't want a third session. I couldn't do that again with you without falling for you."

"I've already fallen," I murmur, my lips coming dangerously close to touching hers.

"What are you saying?" Her breath is a warm pant against my mouth.

"You might have said this was just sex, but you're about to get a whole lot more, because if we do this, there will be no going back."

"Reece?"

"I want a real shot with you. I want to tell Hale everything. I want to make up for not being there for you for the past six years, and I'll fight for you if I have to. I want to protect you, cherish you, own you . . ." The words pour from me, and once they're out, a wave of panic swims through me. Macey doesn't say anything, and the seconds tick past.

Leaning closer, she breathes out, "Will you make love to me?"

When her lips barely brush mine, I have to physically restrain myself from taking her mouth and fucking it with my tongue. Reminding myself that her brother is still watching from inside does the trick.

I force a deep breath into my lungs. "I want to bury myself balls deep inside your sweet body. I want to fuck you for hours. Days. Months. Years."

"Years?" Her lips twitch with a small smile. "I might get a little sore."

"Then I'll tend to your every ache and pain, soothe every discomfort. You will be mine."

Tears spring to her eyes, and she blinks them away.

"Hey, what is it?" I whisper.

"I've waited so long for this. This is the version of you I've missed and dreamed about for six years."

Pleasure swims through me, and my heart feels whole again. "I'm here."

"I thought I lost you," she whispers.

"I'm back." I tug the blanket higher over her shoulders and press a kiss to her forehead. "Can I take you home?"

"Please."

We head inside to join Hale and Brielle in the kitchen. I hold her hand the entire time, a distinct sign of ownership, and Hale reacts accordingly, watching me closely with a scowl slashed across his face. I know I'll have to prove myself to him, and I intend to. However long it takes.

"I'm going to take Macey home." My voice is firm.

Macey hugs Brielle, and then tells her brother good-bye. Hale shoots me evil glares the entire time.

"Are you sure that's a good idea, sis?" he asks.

"Stop it, Cameron. I've forgiven Reece. You need to too."

Hearing her say she's forgiven me is like a shot of adrenaline. "I'm going to do things right this time," I say, looking him square in the eye. I have no idea what that means or what comes next, but I know I can't continue living as the man I was.

"Don't fuck it up," he says sternly, tugging Brielle tightly to his side.

"Wouldn't dream of it." I give Macey's hand a squeeze and we head toward the door. It feels like I'm walking toward my future, and the significance of this moment isn't lost on me.

After I help her inside my car and crank up the heater, we sit there quietly for a moment, as if we're unwilling to break the silence just yet. I have zero expectations of anything happening between us tonight since I'm pretty certain I have to rebuild her trust in me. I'm not sure what that might involve, but I'm thinking proper dates, roses for no reason, handwritten notes telling her all the things I love about her. And time. Time to prove that I'm here for the long haul, and I won't leave or send her away again.

I put the car into gear, then realize I'm unsure how to get to her apartment. "What's your address?"

She turns to look at me, a mischievous glint in her eye. "I thought we'd go to your place."

"You want to go to Crave?"

She shrugs. "I think we've waited long enough, don't you?"

Hearing those words spill from her mouth ignites something inside me. They encapsulate everything I've felt. Placing my hand on the back of her neck, I guide her mouth to mine, and when our lips touch and she releases a small sigh, I almost lose all control. There is so much emotion behind that one little sound. Relief. Desire. Need.

My tongue quests for hers, licking and sucking in a sensual way. Macey moans against me and leans closer. I lift her over the console and place her in my lap, needing her closer still. The heat of her sweet cunt is pressing into my jeans and my cock jumps up, seeking entrance to the forbidden spot I've never allowed myself to go with her. She grinds against me, just as desperate to fuck as I am. My teeth graze her bottom lip as I lift my hips to press against her, stimulating her through her clothes.

"Reece, I want you," she breathes against my mouth.

"You better be sure, Pancake, because once I start, I don't know if I'll be able to stop."

"I've never been more sure about anything."

I want to yell, pump my fist in the air, and jump for joy. Instead I stomp down on the accelerator and get us the hell out of here.

Chapter Fourteen

Macey

When we finally reach Crave, I've never been more impatient to be alone with someone in my entire life. Reece's palm rests against my lower back as he guides me through the club, sending all kinds of territorial signals within me. I love it. His dominant nature only makes him that much more desirable. And knowing he's taking me to his bedroom, instead of his playroom? I'm surprised my panties haven't melted right off my body.

"Are you sure you don't want to stop for a drink?" Reece leans down and whispers near my ear, sending tingles shooting down my spine.

"Stop stalling, Jackson," I tease, and continue straight toward the elevator. I hear him chuckle under his breath as he gives chase.

I press the button for the elevator and wait impatiently. Finally the door opens, and Reece waits for me to step inside before joining me. As the doors slide closed, he stalks closer, pinning me to the wall with his hips.

Holy hell, that's one big erection.

"I should fuck you right here." He presses the hard bulge against my belly.

"I would have zero objections to that." I feel desired and sexy when I'm near him.

His hands skim down my sides and grasp my hips firmly. "No. I need you in my bed. I need to take my time and do this right."

Chills rake down my body. Knowing he doesn't bring women to his bedroom, that he doesn't allow himself the intimacy of it, makes this even more special.

Finally, we enter his apartment and I follow Reece inside. He doesn't turn on any lights, leaving the dim glow of moonlight and the city street lamps from outside to create ambient lighting.

He pauses in the foyer, and I'm at a loss for

what to do. I thought he'd lead me into his bedroom, rip my clothes from my body, and fuck me senseless, but instead he's looking at me with complete love and adoration in his eyes. I'm beginning to realize this is much more than just sex with my old flame. This is my future, my heart, my soul, my everything. If he's just going to walk away after, leave me alone again, I won't be able to handle it.

He stalks closer, pinning me with his gaze. "Come here, beautiful. You're mine tonight."

Tonight. That's what I'm afraid of. He doesn't have the best track record of sticking around.

"I need a minute," I blurt, then break away and head for the bathroom, locking the door behind me.

Shit. Shit. Shit.

I consider calling Brielle to ask her what I should do, but I realize I left my purse in the front entryway, my cell phone inside it.

Frustrated, I pace in the small bathroom—two steps one way, then two back. The scent of his aftershave hangs in the air, deep notes of sandalwood and crisp spruce that only make me ache for him more. *Shit.*

Reece's footsteps approach from down the hall. Three gentle taps on the door startle me.

"Macey? Are you okay?"

He must think I'm nuts. I clench my hands tightly at my side, angry at myself for being such a coward. "No. Yes. I mean, I think so."

"Are you sick?" His voice rises with concern.

"No."

"Changed your mind?"

"I don't know. Maybe." I place one trembling hand over my mouth, trying to sort out the mess of feelings inside me.

A deep sigh sounds from the other side of the door. "You owe it to me to at least come out here and tell me what the hell's going on."

I take a deep breath, trying to work up the

courage to face him. When I unlock the door, I'm standing face-to-face with Reece. His expression is angry, and I'm guessing we're about to get into a heated debate. My stomach twists into a painful knot. I knew his kind words, his sweet kisses had all been too good to be true. He was only in this for the sex, and now that I've changed my mind, he's done. He doesn't do relationships, so what did I expect?

"I know what this is. I know what you're doing," he says, his voice tense.

"Then please fucking explain it to me. I want you. I want this. I'm just . . ."

"I know." He takes my hand and guides me into his bedroom, which smells even more like him. It's intoxicating, and makes my head spin.

We sit down on the bed. He says nothing for a moment, just continues holding my hands, his thumb softly caressing the back of my fingers as he looks at me with sympathy that I don't understand.

"Will you please tell me what's going on?" I beg.

"It's called the flight-or-fight response. It's human nature. When faced with a new concept, a dangerous animal, or a potentially life-changing situation, it's a natural response to want to duck for cover. To protect yourself at all costs. You lost your parents at a young age, then we were separated for many years, and most recently your ex-douche cheated on you."

"What are you talking about? I need you to start making sense. This has nothing to do with my parents or Tony." I resist the urge to roll my eyes. He must think I'm insane.

"Pancake, I'm sorry to tell you this, but it has everything to do with that." He laces his fingers with mine and gazes into my eyes. "It's okay to be scared. This is a big step for us. It's something we've both wanted for years, and now that it's about to happen, it's okay to feel apprehensive."

"It is?" I tilt my head, my eyes narrowing on his.

"Absolutely."

"Gosh, I feel like an idiot. Here we are about to have sex, and I completely ruin the mood by acting like a girl. You must hate me."

"I could never hate you. Quite the opposite, actually." He leans in close and presses a tender kiss to my lips.

"I don't deserve this." His kindness and understanding when I've basically just cut and run is sweet.

"Of course you do. Don't say that." He presses a kiss to my forehead, and I almost melt at how sweet he's being. "This is a big step for us, and I've told you there will be no going back to being friends once we cross this line. So you have a big decision to make. You know what I want. If you decide to let me in, unconsciously you know that losing me would hurt you all over again."

I take a minute to process everything he's said. I don't know when he got so wise, but I know in my heart he's completely right. My mini meltdown in the bathroom? It's because I'm terrified of losing him again.

Staring at our joined hands, I give his a squeeze. "After sex, are you going to leave?"

"No. Fuck no. That just about killed me last time leaving you alone in my playroom."

Sweet relief floods through me. That almost killed me too.

"We'll take this at whatever pace you need to. I want you, badly." His gaze dips down to the front of his pants, where *geez*, that looks painful. His dick is trying to burst through the zipper. "But I want you to be ready and feel comfortable. I'll wait however long I need to. I'm not going anywhere."

Realizing he's just said the exact words I needed to hear to feel comfortable, my libido returns, reminding me that I've wanted every inch of him for years. I lean into his touch, longing to experience the physical feel of his love.

"I can't wait one more minute to have those

sweet lips on mine again, though," he whispers, bringing his mouth to mine. "Is this okay?" He strokes my hair, gazing at me with such love in his eyes, it's impossible not to feel wanted.

"Yes," I breathe, waiting for him to kiss me.

And he does. Just a light press of his lips to mine at first, then his teeth graze my lower lip and his tongue sweeps against mine. Then he's kissing me the way I remember from my best memories. His tongue coaxes mine; his mouth hot and needy, moves over mine. I grow warm all over and my panties get damp. It's never been this good with anyone else.

Growing bold and unable to resist, I slide my hand upward from where it's been resting on his firm thigh. My fingers brush the straining erection that I'm dying to touch. When Reece doesn't react, other than to continue to kiss me with deep stokes of his tongue, I give his cock a squeeze. A grunt escapes him, and my panties flood with moisture.

"Careful, Pancake," he says, breaking his lips

from mine. "I'm trying to be good here, and it's taking all the restraint I have not to strip you naked and fuck you raw."

"Do you remember what I said to you that first night I showed up here?" I ask, feeling daring.

"Of course I do."

"I wanted hot, sweaty sex."

"And now?" he asks.

"I just want you."

The look of wonder reflected in his eyes almost undoes me. "Then come here." He rises from the bed. "Stand up for me."

I do as I'm told, sensing I've somehow just flipped his Dom switch.

"I want to see all of you, and worship this sexy-as-fuck body the way it deserves."

At his words, my heart rate kicks up speed. I'll be exposed in more way than one tonight. This man will own me after this, quite literally.

He tugs my shirt up and I lift my arms, allowing him to pull it off. Reece leans down and kisses the tops of each breast that are lifted high in my lacy push-up bra. When he reaches behind me and flicks the clasp, I'm already anticipating all the amazing things he's going to show my body tonight.

"Let me see you, beautiful," he whispers.

He kisses my neck as he slides the bra from my body. It drops to the floor between us, and Reece's loving gaze caresses me. He brings his hands to my breasts, and my nipples harden as he strokes me. I can't help but think of our first playroom encounter when he invited Oliver in.

"Did that bother you . . . that first night when Oliver joined us?" Reece asks, as if he's just read my mind.

"No, it didn't bother me, because I knew you wouldn't let things go too far."

"You trusted me," he says with wonder.

I nod. This makes him happy, because he kisses

my lips softly and then drops his head to suck on my breast, circling his tongue around my nipple before sucking it into the warmth of his mouth.

I push my hands into his hair, and my eyes slip closed. I can honestly say I've never been with a man who devotes such thorough attention to my body without expecting anything in return. When his fingers tug at the button of my jeans, I help him by wiggling my hips while he tugs down my pants. Soon they're in a heap on the floor with my shirt and bra. I stand before him in just my panties, as flashbacks to our younger years and our early experimentation flash through my brain.

"I love these, for the record," he says, cupping my breasts again and lightly caressing them.

Smiling at him, I run my fingers down the length of his muscled arm. "And I love your tattoos."

There's a lot of the L-word being thrown around, and while neither of us has actually said those three little words yet, that's exactly what this feels like. It doesn't feel like sex; it feels like love. In the best possible way.

He kisses me once more, and this time his hands go to work on his own pants, unbuttoning them and shoving them to the floor. When I look down, I see the broad head of this cock peeking from the waistband of his black boxer briefs. Those really do a poor job of containing him.

"I think you need bigger underwear," I tease, touching the tip of him.

He smirks. "Or a smaller cock."

I shake my head at him, smirking right back. "I've been dying to get my hands on this. You're not going to restrain me this time, are you?"

"Not a chance in hell. I can't wait to feel your hands on me."

I love his honesty.

Sinking to my knees, I slowly peel his boxers down and his cock springs free. Blinking up at him,

I lean forward and drag my tongue up his steely shaft, loving the masculine taste of him and the way he draws in a sharp inhale.

"What are you doing?" His voice is strained.

"Making you feel good. How do you like it?"

The vein at the base of his neck throbs. "Grip me with your hand."

I curl my fist around him and note how my fingers don't meet.

"And now stroke me."

My hand moves up and down.

"Suck me deep."

Opening my mouth as wide as I can, I lean forward and take him. As soon as my lips close around him, he shudders and his muscular thighs tremble.

"Hell yeah," he groans. "Just like that."

I continue my work on him and feel myself getting wet. It's such a turn-on knowing that I'm bringing this big, beautiful man to his knees.

"Pancake . . ." He groans like he's in pain, and I almost chuckle.

Opening my eyes, I glance up at him with my mouth full. He's thrusting his hips forward in time with my strokes, and the expression on his face is pure bliss.

"That feels fucking incredible."

Pride surges inside me, but before I can continue, his hands are under my arms, lifting me to my feet and tossing me on the bed.

"Now it's my turn," he growls, and crawls toward me.

Chapter Fifteen

Reece

Macey's working my cock like a stripper works a pole.

I can't believe how fast she brings me to the brink of losing control. Our first time in my playroom, I convinced myself that it was just some teenage fantasy, that she didn't really hold this power over me. And then she touched me and I almost embarrassed myself. There's just something about her; there always has been. And now, finally, I get to make her mine.

Staring down, I watch as her full mouth takes my cock, her saliva coating me, her tongue tracing the vein that runs down the length. She's sexy as hell doing this, but I want more.

I grip her arms and tug her up. She's dazed and disoriented when I toss her onto the waiting mattress. "Now it's my turn."

As I crawl toward her, Macey starts to push her panties down her hips until I stop her.

"Don't tell me you're resurrecting your old rule about these staying on," she huffs.

I smirk. "For old time's sake. Humor me, Pancake."

She pouts and is about to protest when I rip a hole in the center of her panties, exposing her bare cunt, glistening beautifully with her wetness. It's a pretty sight.

"What are you doing?" She rises on her elbows to peer down at me and her now-ruined underwear with a hole in the center.

"Something I should have done a long time ago." It's the truth. I should have made love to her all those years ago and made her mine.

Leaning over her on the bed, I bring my nose to her pussy and inhale. Macey squirms. "You smell so fucking good." My cock swells even more. Then I take her clit in my mouth and suck.

She curses and thrusts her hands into my hair, her hips lifting to match the movement of my tongue.

Dragging my tongue up and down her wet center, I find a rhythm that makes her cry out. I know she won't last long, and that's fine with me, because my cock aches so bad, it's weeping. Macey pants and arches her back. Her cries are getting more desperate, and I want to push her over the edge. Easing one finger inside her, I curl it upward and stroke the spot I know will set her off. Her fingernails rake against my scalp, and I give her clit a tiny nip with my teeth.

She comes hard, grinding herself against my face without shame. I love how she takes her pleasure so unapologetically. A lot of women want to be dainty and well-mannered about it, but Macey is loud. She curses and pulls my hair, and I fucking love that about her. Watching her lose control is my new favorite thing. I need to make her do that over and over again. But not right now, because if I don't get inside her in the next minute, I might explode.

She's lying on her back with her dark hair spilling over my pillow, her breasts rising and falling with each sharp breath. And her white, lacy panties are torn in the perfect spot. If I hadn't been so afraid to get close to her, this is where I would have brought her that first night. To my bed, where we can curl together afterward and sleep.

I kneel between her parted knees. Just knowing that I'm about to feel her for the first time without a barrier of protection between us, it's indescribable. My heart is just as exposed. This will change everything, and the way she's looking up at me with those stunning blue eyes of hers, I know she can feel it too. The electricity in the air around us is filled with anticipation and desire and love.

I plant one hand on her hip, and the other traces whisper-soft circles on her inner thigh. Her legs fall open, exposing her to me.

Part of me wants to take my time and savor this, and the other part of me is screaming at me to get inside her as quickly as possible.

Leaning closer, I touch the head of my cock to her opening, and Macey flinches. Her reaction is unexpected. "Just try and breathe for me, okay?"

"Will it fit?" she asks, her voice soft.

"It'll fit," I promise her.

She pulls her bottom lip between her teeth, frowning before she says, "I've never been with anyone as big as you before."

Her words should fill me with male pride, but she looks genuinely worried. My brows draw together, and I'm filled with concern. "Be still okay?"

She gives a quick nod.

It feels a little strange, examining her this way, but I want her to be ready for this, and not apprehensive. Bringing two fingers to her opening, I slowly push them inside. My hands are large, but my cock will be much thicker. Her pussy is tight around my fingers, but she stretches for me. "How does that feel?"

She moans, and her expression changes from worry to pleasure.

I work my fingers in and out until I feel her on the brink of another orgasm.

"Baby, if I don't get inside you soon . . ." I grip the base of my cock and squeeze. Macey's eyes zero in on the movement and she groans.

"Yes, please. Inside me. I'm ready," she moans.

Gripping my shaft, I bring the head of my cock to her opening. Macey watches me with wide eyes. And fuck, I can't take my eyes off of her either.

I consider removing the torn remnants of her panties, but something in me likes the nostalgia. Plus, it's pretty fucking hot seeing the torn hole in her panties allows me just enough room to fit the head of my dick against her.

With each thrust, I press into her just a little deeper.

She groans and grips my thighs, her fingers fighting for something to hold on to.

I can't imagine how this feels for her, but for me, it's incredible. She fits around me as tight as a glove. "Breathe," I say. "Just a little bit more."

Putting my hands under her ass, I spread her. She's stretched to her limit, but it fits. I grind against her, burying myself balls deep, and Macey whimpers.

"Tell me if it gets to be too much, okay?"

She nods, her eyes squeezed closed.

"Look at me."

When she opens them, two endless pools of blue latch onto mine.

"Just stay with me, okay?"

She nods again, this time watching my movements as I push my cock in and out of her. Now she's soaking wet, and I slide in and out with ease.

Done being gentle, I pound into her again and again, knowing if I'm not careful, I'll fuck her raw. I need to show some restraint, but all my perfect control is gone. Macey writhes beneath me, matching my thrusts with her pelvis angled toward mine to take as much of me as she can.

It's better than I ever could have imagined.

The pressure is incredible. The sensation is like a warm, wet hug. When I bring my hand to her clit and massage her there again, her inner muscles clench down around me.

This is it. Macey bites her lip and closes her eyes.

"No way," I tell her. "Open them. Let me watch you come."

With another slow, deep drive within her, I feel Macey begin to come. Her body trembles, and she cries out as pleasure over takes her.

Her pussy grips me, sucking at me, and I couldn't pull away right now if my life depended on it.

Her release triggers my own. She milks me, my come coming in long spurts inside her. I've never come inside a woman before without a condom, and it's by far the most erotic thing I've ever done. I love that I shared it with Macey.

Leaning down, I kiss her temple and hug her body close to mine. "I love you," I whisper.

Her breathing stops for a moment, as though she's surprised, and then she takes in a breath and whispers, "I love you too."

Chapter Sixteen

Reece

"There's just one thing I still don't understand," I say, watching Macey. She and I are standing in the lounge of the club, enjoying a cocktail together. It's Saturday night, and the sexual energy swamping the room is palatable.

She takes a sip of her drink and gazes up at me over the rim. "What's that?"

"How in the world did Tony end up in bed with Pinky?" I ask, tucking a strand of loose hair behind her ear and treating her to a smirk.

Macey gives a short bark of laughter. "Seriously?"

I love that we're confident enough in our relationship now, we can discuss things like this openly. "There has to be a story there." I shrug.

"Who the hell knows," Macey scoffs, but there's humor in her voice. "She was our landlord, and lived just upstairs. Since he wasn't working, they began hanging out during the day. I guess their friendship just evolved from there."

"He's a fucking idiot." I take a drink of my own cocktail and thank my lucky stars that Tony fucked up the way he did. "Why did they call her Pinky?"

She shrugs. "She had a chunk of blond hair that had been dyed pink near her temple."

"I'm so glad you figured out what a douche bag he was, and that you're here now."

She smiles at me warmly. "Me too."

One of the servers stops by to ask if we'd like another drink. We both decline and share a heated look, knowing where our evening is headed. I want to be fully sober when I lead her into the scene we're going to share tonight.

To say that my staff is shocked I have a girlfriend would be the understatement of the century. Over the last several weeks, Macey and I have grown closer, and tonight, we're ready to explore the club together. We haven't been in my private room since we started dating, and I considered clearing the room of my personal effects and turning it back over to the general club population to use. But when I mentioned that to Macey, she frowned. She didn't like that our last memories there were sour ones, and I knew that I needed to fix that.

As we're finishing our drinks, Oliver and Chrissy wander up. The club is in full swing tonight, and I know they'll both be busy with clients later.

"Hey, boss," Chrissy says, leaning in to give me a quick hug, and then gives one to Macey too. She and Macey have developed a friendship over the past few weeks, and I've been pleasantly surprised by that. There's been no jealousy, no cattiness, and no weird feelings. Oliver, on the other hand, is a different story. Macey blushes and stammers whenever he's near. I think it might take her some time to accept that this man saw her naked and participated in a scene with us. Well, briefly anyway.

"Evening, Macey," Oliver says, stopping beside her. He towers over her, and Macey shrinks back a step closer to me.

"Hi," she squeaks. My normally confident firecracker is subdued in his presence. Chrissy exchanges a curious stare with me, obviously wondering what's going on.

"Can I speak with you privately for a minute?" Oliver asks Macey.

She glances to me, gauging my reaction. "Go ahead, Pancake," I tell her. Oliver's got a way with words, and perhaps speaking with her alone will help her finally get over this awkwardness between them.

Chrissy and I watch as they walk away, heading toward the semi-private lounge area. Macey glances back at me, and I give her a slight nod of encouragement.

"What's that about?" Chrissy asks, watching them where they sit together on a loveseat. Oliver is speaking in hushed tones, and Macey's nodding along to whatever he's saying.

I shrug. Chrissy likes to be in the know on club business, and normally I don't mind that, but this isn't club business—it's personal. "Who knows," I say. "You know Oliver. I'm sure he's just sharing some bit of wisdom with her."

"He is intuitive," she says. "But it doesn't take a rocket scientist to see that you two are happy and in love." She smiles at me. "It's nice to see."

"Yeah." It *is* nice. "It's been a long time coming." Six long years I waited for Macey to come back into my life. And now that I have her, I'm never letting her go. A concept Hale's still getting used to.

Moments later, Macey and Oliver head back our way, and it's obvious their talk helped. Macey's gait is lighter, and a small smile adorns her lips as she strolls to my side.

"Come on, Chrissy," Oliver says. "We've got clients to entertain."

Macey and I watch them walk away into the depths of the club.

"Everything okay?" I kiss the top of her head as she nestles in against me.

"Perfectly fine."

"What did he say?"

"He told me more about his role here, and that it really wasn't something out of the ordinary for him to be in a room with a couple, and not to make more of it than it was."

I've told her the same thing three times. "That's it?"

She nods. "And he said if it would help, he would let me see him naked too. Even the score, you know."

"Not happening, sweetheart."

She scoffs. "Even if that's what I needed to feel

better about the situation?"

Narrowing my eyes, I study her. "Is it?"

"Well, no." Her cheeks pinken slightly as she glances away.

I chuckle. "Good." I don't quite know how I'd feel about that now that we're exclusively together. I lean down and kiss the sensitive spot behind her ear. "Go into my private room and wait for me on the bed."

"Okay," she says on an exhale.

"I changed the code."

"What is it?" she asks, watching me curiously.

Leaning down to whisper near her ear, I breathe in her scent. Lavender and vanilla, my favorite combination. "Your birthday."

She smiles warmly at me. The truth is, this is not my private room anymore. It's hers. If it weren't for her pouting lip, I would have given up the room. Oliver could use a second therapy room, after all.

Lifting up on her toes, Macey treats me to a

kiss on my cheek and then saunters away, her round hips swaying enticingly as she goes.

It takes all the willpower I have not to chase after her. My cock is already lengthening in my pants. But I want to take my time making love to her tonight. Intimacy and sex was something I withheld from myself for so long, and now that I have the girl I've wanted all along, it's like I'm making up for lost time. We lay entangled together every night, and I bury myself in her once or twice every day just because I can, and still it's not enough.

I wonder if it will ever be enough.

Chapter Seventeen

Macey

Six months later

"You didn't have to do this, you know," I say, stepping out of the limousine and glancing around at the park-like setting.

"Are you kidding? I wanted to. The chance to see you in a sexy-as-hell dress?" Reece's hands skim down my sides, sliding over the silky fabric of the wine-colored dress I'm wearing.

My six-inch heels bring me a little closer to his height, and I only have to rise up on my toes to press my lips to his. We share a deep, passionate kiss before I finally pull away.

"Are you going to tell me what we're doing here?" I ask.

"Come with me."

The driver pulls off into the parking lot in the distance, while Reece takes my hand and guides me over toward the gazebo where he's obviously taken the time to make sure everything would be perfect for our date. Twinkling white lights crisscross from the ceiling, and soft music plays in the background. A bucket of ice waits with a bottle of champagne, and a little farther away is a blanket laid out on a grassy hill under the stars.

"What's all this for?" I smile at him. I'm still not used to the way Reece dotes on me, even after six months of dating.

"We're still catching up on all the things I missed, all the romantic dates I should have taken you on."

"You don't have to do that."

He shakes his head, smirking at me. "Remember when that twerp Jacob took you to prom?"

I grin. "Of course."

"It should have been me. I still regret that I wasn't the one who took you."

As I look around at our surroundings with new eyes—my sexy man dressed in a black suit and tie, me in a formal gown, and the romantic backdrop around us—I realize he's recreating prom just for us. It brings tears to my eyes. If my world hadn't fallen apart in Miami, if I hadn't caught my ex cheating on me, I hate to think if things had been just a little different that I might not be here with the man I love more than anything.

"I thought you and my brother were okay with Jacob." I suppress the urge to roll my eyes when I remember how they approved all my dates back then by joint decision

"I did approve of him, but that doesn't mean that I didn't threaten to neuter him if he laid one fucking finger on you." Reece's expression darkens. "Wait, he didn't touch you, did he?"

"Reece Jackson," I scold. I should let him believe Jacob did, but I'm not that cruel. I wouldn't put it past Reece to go searching for the guy and make good on his promise.

"Tell me," he says.

"No, he behaved like a perfect gentleman all night. By the end of the evening, I was wondering what was wrong with me, and why he didn't find me attractive."

He gives me a smug grin. "There's not a thing wrong with you. I just couldn't have some high school kid touching what was mine."

This time, I do roll my eyes at him.

"You look stunning."

"I'm not wearing any panties, you know."

Reece groans. "Are you trying to kill me?"

"No, I just know you'll probably ruin them." He has a thing for ripping my panties, not that I'm complaining. "Let's go. You owe me a dance under the stars."

The evening is perfect. We sip champagne,

slow dance to the soft jazz floating through the air, and laugh as we reminisce about old times together. It's much better than my first prom.

"You changed your nail color," Reece says, holding my hand. We're sitting on the blanket he arranged under the stars.

My nails are now painted a light pink, and I simply nod. I know he thought my black nails were some kind of reflection on my mood, and maybe they were. I was in a dark place when we first got together. But that's changed.

I have the world's best boyfriend. He has a heart of gold, a huge cock, and intimate knowledge of all the best sex toys. I feel like I've won the damn lottery. When I moved back to Chicago, I was searching for something, and even if I didn't know it at the time, true love was waiting to find me and sweep me off my feet. When I remember how hard Reece fought his feelings for me, it makes my heart hurt. We had a rocky start, but things are good now. They're great, actually. Nana adores him, and even Hale has accepted our relationship.

"Thank you for planning the perfect prom date for us." I lean over and kiss his cheek. His rough stubble and the scent of rugged aftershave greet me, and my heart rate picks up. As long as I live, I will never get enough of him.

"One more dance before we go?" he asks, rising to his feet, and tugging me up against him.

"Yes, but I think I need to take off these heels, if you don't mind."

"Not at all."

I step out of my shoes and kick them to the side. Reece surprises me by lifting me off my feet and spinning me around. When he lowers me to my feet, the grass tickles my bare toes, and we begin sway together. Resting my head on his shoulder, I'm enjoying being totally relaxed and at ease when sense he has other ideas. His cock rises and hardens against my belly, and his fingers move from my hips down to my ass, squeezing.

His mouth moves to my neck, where he lightly

kisses and nibbles at my throat. "Sorry, sweetheart, it seems I can't behave myself around you."

"You don't have to behave." Encouraging him, I tilt my hips toward his to rub against the firm ridge in his suit pants. Soon our dancing resembles groping as we kiss deeply and rub up against each other.

"I need you," he groans against my neck, making my whole body shiver.

"The limo?" There's no way I'm waiting until we're home to feel him inside me.

"I won't make it that long," he growls.

I'm about tell him it's only a hundred-yard walk when he tugs me behind a tree and unbuttons his pants. I watch in stunned fascination as he takes his cock from his pants and begins stroking himself. Then he lifts me, tugging up my dress as he goes, and situates me so my back is against the tree and my legs are wound around his waist.

"Tell me to stop if you don't want this," he says, pausing for a moment to be sure I'm okay with this.

"Fuck me," I say.

And he does. He lines himself up and slowly sinks inside me until I feel like I've been stretched and filled to my breaking point. Consumed by pleasure, I fuse my mouth to his and we kiss deeply, not caring about oxygen, or the fact we're in public.

Hanging onto his shoulders, I love the feel of being in his strong arms, and the way he rocks into me over and over again, setting the perfect pace.

"You. Feel. So. Fucking. Good," he murmurs, burying his face against my neck.

Gripping under my ass, he shoves me up and down on that huge cock of his, massaging me in all the right places. Much too soon, I lose control, my inner muscles clenching around him as I let go.

Reece swears, and thrusts—hard—a final time, his cock swelling within me as he comes.

Afterward, he sets me on my feet and kisses my mouth softly. "That was perfect. Thank you."

The sticky heat of us between my legs tells me a hot shower will be in order when we get home. Realizing I'm now a mess, I'm thankful when Reece drapes his suit jacket over my shoulders and picks up my shoes. Holding hands, we make our way to the limo, still slightly breathless and with impish grins on our lips.

Epilogue

Reece

Shit. I'm pacing around the apartment, double-checking all the light fixtures and that the windows are locked, when I feel Macey's presence behind me.

"What are you doing?" she asks, standing with her hand on her hip.

"Checking for any small choking hazards."

"Behind the curtains? Amelia is three months old. I doubt she'll be crawling around over there."

"When do they crawl?" I ask, stopping my search of possible danger and mayhem.

"Usually around nine months or so," Macey says.

Okay, so I still have a few more months to baby proof. "Sorry, I guess I'm just anxious. I've never babysat before."

Macey smiles warmly. "Come sit down."

I join her on the couch, and try to relax.

"I've babysat lots of times when I was younger, plus we've both spent plenty of time around Amelia."

She's right. I'm sure it'll be fine, it's just that this is a big deal to me. Tonight we're babysitting for Hale and Brielle so they can go on their first date night since they had Amelia. She's three months old, and so damn cute. Thank God she looks like her mommy and not her daddy.

There's a knock at the door and I shoot off the couch. "I'll get it."

Macey chuckles at me as I head for the door.

Hale has two diaper bags strapped to him, along with Brielle's purse, and he looks a little worried. I would be too if I was about to leave a kid with me. Brielle, on the other hand, appears calm and collected as she gently bounces their daughter, Amelia, in her arms.

"I'll take her." Brielle smiles and hands Amelia over to me. "Hi, princess." I look down at her at coo. Her blue eyes light up and she smiles a gummy grin at me.

Macey stands beside me and looks down at the baby.

Brielle strokes her hand through Amelia's dark hair and smiles. "She needs her bottle at about seven, and then we change her and lay her down by eight."

"Okay, bottle at seven, diaper at . . . maybe we should write this down," I say.

"I'll remember," Macey assures me, sharing an amused look with Brielle.

Hale begins pulling items from his bag. "This is her favorite dolly. And her binky is the purple one with the princess crown on it." He hands me a cloth baby doll in a pink dress. "And she likes to be rocked to sleep with her blankie tucked around her."

"Got it. What about diapers?"

Hale rummages around inside the bag. "I packed twelve. You'll probably only need one, but you can never be too prepared."

I nod in silent agreement, trying to soak in every detail. Then I notice Macey and Brielle standing back and gawking at us as if we're the most comical thing they've ever seen.

Two big fucking Doms, and we turn into bumbling idiots around a baby.

Shit.

"It's a baby, not a rocket ship," I say, shrugging my shoulders. "We'll figure it out."

Hale straightens beside me, realizing how we must look to our women. "Right. It'll be fine." He leans in and kisses his daughter's forehead before taking Brielle's hand. "Are you ready?"

She nods. "Thank you guys so much for watching her. We'll only be gone a few hours. And please call me if she gives you any trouble at all."

"Take your time. You guys deserve this break.

Have fun," Macey says, opening the door for them.

When the door closes behind them and I'm left holding a baby in my arms, I'm really glad Macey's here with me.

"What should we do now?" I ask.

"Let's bring her into the living room. We can play for a little bit before it's time for her bottle."

I carry her into the living room, and lay her down on the sofa between Macey and me.

"Will you hand me her baby doll?"

Macey grabs the diaper bag with a confused look on her face. "Didn't Hale have two bags?"

"Uh. I think that second one might have been his toy bag."

Realization dawns and Macey grimaces. "Let's file that under *information I did not need*." She's still frowning when she hands me the doll.

I chuckle and go back to playing with Amelia. "How do you feel about one of these?"

"A baby?" Her confusion is obvious, with a furrowed line appearing between her brows.

"Yeah."

"With you, you mean?"

"I sure as fuck don't want some other guy knocking up my girlfriend, so yes, with me." I grin.

She smiles broadly. "I didn't know you wanted kids."

We hadn't talked about that yet, which only makes me realize there is so much to look forward to in our future. "I do. In fact, I want all of it. Marriage, kids, and a house in the suburbs to raise them in."

"What about the club?"

"The club will always be part of my life, but I've thought about hiring a full-time operations manager to run the place for me down the road. I can be a silent owner. I don't think a BDSM club is a good place to raise a kid. But it could be the perfect place for mommy and daddy to escape to on a date night, don't you think?" I look down at Amelia and chuckle.

"Ew! Are you serious? My brother and Brielle are at the club right now? That's their big date?" Macey shudders, and I just laugh.

After all, adults need playtime too.

Author's Note

Thank you so much for taking the time to read *Sinfully Mine*. When I first began writing this story, I wasn't quite sure where it ended. I knew that despite their pasts, Macey and Reece were no longer afraid to love and had grown considerably as a couple. But as I got closer to the final chapter, I knew it had to end where it all started—with Hale and Brielle sharing the scene, and showcasing the significant emotional growth of our two leading men.

Hale and Reece have each settled into their roles as caring, possessive alpha males focused on family and love, rather than Dominants focused on life's carnal pleasures. It was fun to envision them as happy family men, although the scenes where they explored their more base, carnal natures were fun to write too.

If you haven't checked out *The Gentleman Mentor* yet, I hope that you do so you can enjoy

Hale and Brielle's story as well.

About *The Gentleman Mentor*

He calls himself the Gentleman Mentor.

Just reading his ad makes me feel more alive than I have in years. He promises to teach me the art of seduction, and show me the most sinfully erotic pleasures. He's going to help me become the kind of confident, sexy woman men can't ignore. Six lessons with the most gorgeous man ... who happens to be a Dom. The only problem is that now that I've experienced his brand of delectable domination, will anyone else ever compare?

She's a client; that's all.

Or it should be. But with every lesson, she's becoming more. The secrets I'm hiding behind the image of the Gentleman Mentor make telling her the truth—and having anything real—impossible. I'm training her for another man, and that fact guts me every time I think of it. I know she's not mine, but part of me won't accept that. Am I willing to risk it all to keep her?

Praise for *The Gentleman Mentor*

"Totally unexpected and intriguing. With a unique storyline that had me engrossed from page one. This is a Kendall Ryan book you won't want to miss!" – *#1 New York Times Bestselling Author, Rachel Van Dyken*

"These are the kinds of lessons you'll want to study over and over again. Ryan is a master at building sweltering seduction and poignant longing between the novice and the mentor. This scorching romance will leave the reader with the clear reminder that we all have a little something left to learn." – *Jay Crownover, New York Times bestselling author*

"The gentleman has a dirty, dirty mouth!!" – *Cocktails and Books Blog*

"A hot, sexy, and kinky read." – *Carissa,* Goodreads *Reviewer*

concession I agreed to, and one that's never

Acknowledgments

A hearty thank-you to Pam Berehulke, Danielle Sanchez, Angela Smith, and Rachel Brookes. You each play a significant role in helping me on my writing journey. Each novel is different, some more difficult than others, so thank you for being there to support me.

To all of the bloggers, fans, and readers who have shared my books with others, who've left reviews and made beautiful graphic teasers, my heart is filled with bookish love for you. I hope you know how critical you are to this community. I'm grateful for every tweet, review, and mention. My readers mean everything to me, and I'm blessed to have your support.

To my little family. You're everything to me.

About the Author

Kendall Ryan is the *New York Times*, *USA TODAY*, and *Wall Street Journal* bestselling author of more than a dozen contemporary romance novels including *Hard to Love, Resisting Her, When I Break*, and the Filthy Beautiful Lies series. Her books have been published into multiple languages and are sold in more than fifty countries around the world.

She loves reading about tough alpha heroes with a sweet side, and aims to capture that in her writing. She detests laundry and enjoys coffee, cupcakes, and being outdoors, playing with her two infant sons and darling husband.

Other Books by Kendall Ryan

UNRAVEL ME Series:
Unravel Me
Make Me Yours

LOVE BY DESIGN Series:
Working It
Craving Him
All or Nothing

WHEN I BREAK Series:
When I Break
When I Surrender
When We Fall
When I Break (complete series)

FILTHY BEAUTIFUL LIES Series:
Filthy Beautiful Lies
Filthy Beautiful Love
Filthy Beautiful Lust
Filthy Beautiful Forever

LESSONS WITH THE DOM Series:
The Gentleman Mentor

Stand-alone Novels:
Hard to Love
Reckless Love
Resisting Her
The Impact of You

CPSIA information can be obtained at www.ICGtesting.com
Printed in the USA
LVOW11s1824171016

509105LV00004B/909/P